INKED IN VENGEANCE

Royal Bastards MC: New Orleans Chapter

CRIMSON SYN

Cover by Jay Aheer
Photography done by Eric Battershell
Cover Model: Drew Truckle

❀ Created with Vellum

DEAR READERS

I have to admit that I have never had so much fun on a project, like I have in this one. The Royal Bastards is such an important series to me. An idea that literally was meant to be for fun, flourished into an amazing new MC world. And I have to say, we couldn't have done it without you, our readers. You have been amazingly supportive and enthusiastic through this whole process and we appreciate each and every single one of you for taking time out to indulge in stories.

I want to say a huge thank you to the people who made this possible, and to every single author who graced this series with their amazing words: Nikki Landis, for being my other half and sharing this idea with me, my PA, who worked her ass off, and to be honest, I couldn't do this without her, Kristin Youngblood. My fabulously twisted besties CM Genovese, Sean Moriarty & Izzy Sweet-I've never had so much fun planning crimes like I have with you. BB Blaque, Linny Lawless, Kristine Allen, KE Osborn, KL Ramsey, Winter Travers, Elle Boon, Addison Jane, J.Lynn Lombard, Ker Dukey, and K Webster. Thank you so much for lending me your characters and sharing all your incredible plots and ideas with me. Our readers truly have no idea the type of roller coaster ride we're about to take them on.

Elizabeth Knox, thank you for always being on top of things and for all your help, I hope I did your Gamble justice. Glenna Maynard, thank you for always being there for all the authors and for being so absolutely supportive. Your work does not go unnoticed. To Jax Hart, Bink Cummings, Sapphire Knight, Shannon Youngblood, Chelle C Craze, Eli Abbott, Erin Trejo, M. Merin, and my girl, Madison Faye. You all are so unbelievably talented and I thank you for helping me show the world what it means to collaborate, and what you can accomplish when you work together. And to Esther E Schmidt, for having Petros send Sadie to Jameson, thank you. I have to admit, he had a helluva time with her. I couldn't have asked for a better group of authors to work with. Thank you for your time, for your patience, for all that you do. I am so honored to share this series with you.

To my readers, this is Jameson's book. We first met our National Chapter President back in my Death Row Shooters series where he helps Poe with his mission out in Hong Kong. His story begins only a few days after the events that take place with Poet, and he's making sure that his friend gets his justice.

Heed the warning: Jameson is not nice by any means. He shows no remorse for any vengeance he inflicts and he is not one to give compassion. He's suffered great pain and in that pain he dwells. He's brutal, cold, and calculating, and hopefully he'll make you squirm in your seats.

Now, without further adieu, here's Inked In Vengeance.

Sinful Reading,
   Crimson Syn

ROYAL BASTARDS MC

ROYAL BASTARDS CODE

PROTECT: The club and your brothers come before anything else, and must be protected at all costs. **CLUB** is **FAMILY**.

RESPECT: Earn it & Give it. Respect club law. Respect the patch. Respect your brothers. Disrespect a member and there will be hell to pay.

HONOR: Being patched in is an honor, not a right. Your colors are sacred, not to be left alone, and **NEVER** let them touch the ground.

OL' LADIES: Never disrespect a member's or brother's Ol'Lady. **PERIOD.**

CHURCH is MANDATORY.

LOYALTY: Takes precedence over all, including well-being.

HONESTY: Never **LIE, CHEAT,** or **STEAL** from another member or the club.

TERRITORY: You are to respect your brother's property and follow their Chapter's club rules.

TRUST: Years to earn it...seconds to lose it.

NEVER RIDE OFF: Brothers do not abandon their family.

GLOSSARY OF TERMS

Belle Femme: *Beautiful female*

Beau Diable: *Handsome devil*

bèt seksyèl: *beautiful creature*

Papa Legba: *A spirit in Haitian Vodou, who stands at a spiritual crossroads and gives (or denies) permission to speak with the spirits in the spirit world.*

Lwa or Loa: *Spirits of Haitian Vodou and Louisiana Voodoo.*

Ezilie: *Queen of Love, beauty, romance, and riches: life as it should be. She is the most beautiful of the lwa. ... She stimulates and epitomizes love that transcends death.*

ROYAL BASTARDS MC

PROLOGUE

JAMESON

3 Months Ago...

"Qiiing," snot and drool dripped down his chin as he slivered out a plea in his native tongue.

Gripping him by the hair, I lifted his head, dragging the edge of the blade down his cheek. Blood seeped through and I grinned as he whined and howled.

"Did you think things would change when you got back?" His eyes started to fall shut and I slapped him a couple times to no avail.

"Too soon to faint on me," grabbing a bucket of cold water, I threw it in his face and he sputtered and flailed like a marionette on strings.

The position I had him in was uncomfortable at best. Bent over, ropes wrapped around his wrists, arms spread, ankles cuffed and his legs spread. His balls hung heavy and low, and I traced them with the knife, nipping at them. He screamed in agony and I only laughed as blood continued to pool at his feet.

"You think you have all the power, don't you? How do you

feel now Dragon?" I whispered in his ear as I stabbed him along his torso. Small short jabs that wouldn't penetrate any major organs. No, he had to pay for what he did to my friend and his woman.

His gargled pleas meant nothing to me, and I signaled at the door to bring them in once again. They had a field day with him yesterday, today would be equally as enjoyable. One of the men came forward, his tiny cock already erect and ready to defile.

Hong Kong's red district existed for vile shit like this. Rape fantasies ran down the boulevard and businessmen sitting in cubicles all day, such as this one, loved to eat this shit up. I, in turn, made a decent profit from their perversions.

Dragon here had played out his fantasies on my friend Poet, and although the Death Row Shooters had dealt with this sister, they let this fucker go as a warning. Problem is, he landed right at my doorstep. I dragged him out of his house with nothing but his dirty underwear on, and I brought him here. My own little playhouse in the underworld of Hong Kong.

When I first got here, they told me that if you want to survive there are only two ways of doing things. You either become one of the Triads or you pay them off. I don't belong to anyone, least of all will I pay them for it. Instead, I provide what they like most, a dick to suck, and a fresh hole to fuck. No questions asked. And they tend to leave me alone for the most part. But this, this was going to cost me dearly. Because when they find out I killed their Dragon, all of Hong Kong will come looking for me.

The Prince wailed as another male came in and fucked him through and through, and yet another began to break him open once again. Blood continued to pool on the floor, his face growing pale. He deserved it, for touching my family. He didn't deserve to live for what he did to Poe Chambers. The Death Row Shooters, Road Captain, had come here to do business, and this piece of shit took it out on him and his girl. His sister had recently paid that debt, but I didn't take shit like this lightly. There was no way in hell, the Dragon piece of shit would not pay for the damage he'd done.

Poe was one of the only true friends that remained. He saved my life a long time ago and he sent me off to safety. More like sent me off to a shit hole, but you can make of it what you will. I needed somewhere to hide. And Hong Kong was the perfect city to get lost in.

The man grunted and wheezed as I stepped up to him while a reprieve was given. His cock was jutted out and I grimaced. "Are you enjoying this you fucking pervert!" I swung my blade across his ball sack, and he screamed before falling limp, while more blood seeped out onto the floor.

"I'm going to enjoy watching you bleed to death," I whispered in his ear before knocking on the door and letting another man in.

This is what I am. A seeker of retribution. The devil's advocate for vengeance, my own still hiding in the wings. Waiting until my time would come. I stepped aside to let the next man do his business while the Dragon moaned in pain.

The phone rang, taking my attention away, and wiping my bloodied hands on a dirty cloth, I walked over to the wall and picked it up. The man on the other line held a heavy accent. "You got a long-distance phone call. His name is Taron Brown."

It surprised me at first and I frowned, that name bringing back memories. Phone calls that came down here usually came with a recommendation. It was always a member of the triads looking for some fun and games, or just a little help in catching someone. But never a personal call.

And besides, what the hell was a Royal Bastard calling me for, and how did he track me down?

"I'll take it."

There was silence on the line but I could hear him breathing. "You want to tell me how the fuck you found me?"

"Been a long time, Elrik."

"I could say the same to you. Last thing I heard, you were in jail?"

"Still am."

"How'd you find me?"

"I have my ways."

"There are only two people in this world who know where I am. Ian Braxton or Poe Chambers, which one of those fuckers gave me up?"

"We debated who was going to tell you. Ian is busy with his own shit down in New Mexico, so you got me."

I grimaced, and a deep low menacing rumble came out. "What do you want, Knuckles?"

"Hey, don't fucking shoot the messenger. I was told to call you."

"By whom?"

"Colt."

The name struck a chord with me. A deep one. The VP of the New Orleans Chapter had somehow managed to find me. I hadn't heard that name in years and I couldn't say I was pleased to hear it. My grip tightened on the receiver as memories tried to flood in and I stopped them.

"He needs you to come home, Brother."

"He needs me? Where was he when I needed him?" I locked my jaw hearing the receiver crack.

There was silence on the other end. Where Ian and I were able to escape, Knuckles had been one of the members who'd always remained loyal to us. He paid for his loyalty dearly, and there had been nothing I could do about it at the time. When he voted against us leaving, he was stripped of his colors and blamed for aiding and abetting my woman's murder. He was thrown in the State Penitentiary Prison and left there to rot.

From what I could tell, Colt seemed to be the only one to keep in touch with him. Clubhouse rules stated that you never left a brother behind, and if he was down, then you were to take care of him. Seems like they all forgot that rule.

"Why now? What do they want from me?"

"Let's just say that Rancid is about to share a cell block with me."

"What the fuck are you going on about?"

"Rancid's been playing with fire. The FBI has charged him with the murder of sixteen young women, all found in the Bayou behind the clubhouse."

It took me a moment to take in that last bit of information. Rancid was a murderous bastard, but I didn't want him behind bars. No. I wanted him to freely walk the streets. An easier target to play with. Shit just got complicated.

"How'd he get himself locked up?"

"Motherfucker's been working with the Black Market Railroad."

"What the fuck is that?"

"An underground sex trafficking ring that stems from Russia. They've been given the Alaska Chapter a hard time. The FBI took down a branch of these fuckers a while back, and they've been keeping their eye on the waters. Looks like these motherfuckers were swapping girls with Rancid the entire time. They found a girl floating in the bayou right behind the clubhouse. Apparently, they closed the house down, asked questions, and found out he'd been the last one to be seen with her. Word is he's been instrumental in trafficking the Bayou girls into Alaska through Seattle. Don't know how he gets them there, but he's had connections with the Russians for years. Some of these girls have disappeared lately, there have been more than a handful. Group of girls disappears in the Bayou and people start askin' questions round here. Sure enough, the connections were made, and Rancid was taken in."

"Do BP and Rain know what's going on in their territory?"

"I'm sure they do."

"Contact them. If they're in Anchorage then they'll have information. Tell them if they find anything on Rancid and his connections, to send it my way.."

"You plannin' on coming back now that Rancid is in jail?"

I ran my hand through my hair and looked hard down at the concrete. Making that decision was more difficult than I thought. It had been too many years since I'd been discarded by the Royal Bastards. Going back to the people who turned their back on you wasn't something I looked forward to.

"It ain't as easy as you make it seem, Knuckles. There's a lot of people who hate me. I doubt they'd want to see me come back.

"And whoever said you were one to ask for permission. You come in, you take what's yours. It's as simple as that. We were blinded back then, told lies, and after everything was said in done, we paid the price. Because we now know who Rancid's true purpose, and that motherfucker has done a lot of us wrong. He deserves to pay. Besides, Colt says it's time for you to come home."

"And I'm supposed to, what? Follow his fucking orders, now!"

"He wants you to come back and take your rightful place, Brother."

"Stop calling me brother!"

A wail reminded me that I wasn't alone, and when I looked over, one of the pervy fuckers was stroking the Prince's cock as he fucked him. Blood soaked the floor and if it continued, I was gonna lose this prick quickly.

"I need to go."

"Will you at least consider it?"

"I'll think about it."

"Prez..."

The title rang in my ears. I never had the joy of having one of my brothers called me that. That joy was torn away from me along with my soul that night.

"Do you want me to get rid of him for you?"

Another scream escaped the Dragon and he fell limp as cum spurted from his dick mixing with the blood on the floor. The sight of it brought back memories. Sheets splattered in blood, her thighs parted and cum soaked. Her body tied up and lying lifeless on our bed. I closed my eyes and shoved those dark thoughts away.

"No. Make sure he stays alive. That fucker dies by my hand, not in the hands of some gang members. You do what you can to make it known he isn't to be touched. He belongs to me."

"Yes, Sir."

"And Knuckles..."

"Yeah, Prez."

"You're coming home with me."

"Yes, Sir."

I slammed the phone down and walked over to the hanging form. His lips were purple and there wasn't much life to him left. I grabbed him by the hair and pulled his head up, his eyes barely registering me. I traced the knife along his neck and gripping the handle, I sank it sideways into his jugular. He jolted on the ropes, the guy inside him groaning as his body tightened up. He hung there lifeless, as the last man finished, shoving his cock in his pants and walking out.

I cleaned off the blade and called upstairs for a cleanup. By the time they called the Triads to let them know what I'd done to their precious leader, I'd be long gone.

I hugged my jacket tightly around me as I walked out into the brisk Hong Kong polluted air. Slowly I walked down the now familiar streets with their pungent odors and bright neon lights. I made my way home slowly, contemplating everything that had just been thrown at me. It had been a long time since

I'd been back to the states. Six years since they took it all from me. After everything that had gone down, I spent half the time here trying to survive, the rest, waiting for the right time to return. Tonight was it, my opportunity. Rancid would finally pay for all the bad he's caused us. And not just me, or Ian, but all of us.

Rancid was known for raiding clubs, stealing women and titles and destroying everything that crossed his path. When he'd liquidated one club, and stolen all women, contacts, and money, he'd move on to the next. God only knew what he'd done to my father's club. We had twenty-six chapters, I couldn't believe none of them had stepped up. What the fuck had happened to let him continue in his position? Couldn't they see all the wrong he'd done? I'd been so isolated I knew nothing about what was going on. I even lost contact with Ian a few days after I landed. The last I knew he had been taken in by the Nevada Chapter. The Royal Bastards had been my family, the only family I ever knew, and Rancid came and destroyed all that because of envy and greed. But vengeance was mine. It had to be. It had a way of always calling out to me.

The cards had told me that I needed to be patient, that it was almost time. Sneaking out a card from my pocket, I twirled it in my hands. The King of Swords stared back at me, his crown set straight, a sword wielded in his right hand. The tarot was telling me this was it. I had to be calculating and methodical. I was headed back home. To take my throne back and seek revenge on those who did me wrong.

It was time.

8

❦ 1 ❦

JAMESON

THREE WEEKS LATER...

I HAD ONE STOP TO MAKE BEFORE I MADE IT BACK HOME. WHEN I left, I sent a package to an old friend back in New York. one who owed me a favor. F.O.C.U.S. I'm sure he received the package, but I wasn't sure if he'd even want to see me. It had been a long time.

The wind swept around me as I walked the city streets of Midtown Manhattan, dragging along the duffel bag where I'd packed my few belongings. Only the important shit. Clothes on my back, shoes on my feet, and a few personal items I carried with me all the time. A photograph of my father and one of Willow and Ian were kept in my wallet. Everything I needed to survive was in the bag.

New York had its uniqueness. The unforgettable smell of soft pretzels warming up in a nearby cart, or the Nuts 4 Nuts cart that lingered in the corner bringing in the scent of honey roasted almonds. Another half a block and the smell of garbage hit my nose. Cringing, I hastily walked past it, zipping up my leather jacket as the brisk winds of autumn that swept through the building assaulted me at every corner.

The lights up ahead signaled my destination. The Mounds Bar. I nodded at the Prospect at the door and he nodded back. My jacket had no letters on it. I'd stripped myself completely of any patches lest somebody wanted to fuck with me while I traveled alone. Besides, I wasn't sure if I'd ever put them on again. The tattoo on my arm still held the scars of what once was.

Walking through the doors of the strip club, I was greeted at the door by one of the girls. I gave her my name and she grinned at me. Cute, bubbly little redhead. She told me to wait while she made a quick phone call, and then led me through a side door and down a dingy old brick layered hallway before reaching another door. This one led into the Royal Bastards den. A more elegant setting than the club, and much quieter. There were a few girls who lingered around, one in specific sized me up as I walked in. A set of blue-grays that lingered on my crotch.

Go figure.

Standing to the right was Rattler, the club's VP, and Crucifix, the chapter's President. To my left and seated alone in the corner was F.O.C.U.S., the New York Chapter's Sargent At Arms. A bright orange light flickered on, and as he leaned forward he took in a long draw of his cigar.

The silence hung in the air, and for a moment I wasn't sure what I'd just stepped into. It wasn't until Crucifix spoke that I realized I was holding my breath.

"Well, hot damn, if it isn't the devil himself!" He came at me and hauled me into a hug, his hands came around me and I knew he was giving me a good pat-down. Making sure he knew exactly the placement of any weapon I was packin'.

"We weren't expectin' you for another few days."

"I literally just landed."

"Fuck, it's good to see you."

I gave out a half-hearted chuckle before turning to F.O.C.U.S. "I think you know why I'm here, Brother."

"I've got her stored safely."

"You treat her right?"

"I ain't puttin' my life in jeopardy over your Harley. Besides, I owe you."

"You got that job finished back in New Orleans."

"All settled. Satan's Scavenger's got what was coming to them."

"Good to hear."

"Sit." Crucifix led me to one of the couches and sat across from me. Rattler sat to my right, while F.O.C.U.S. sat to my left.

"How you doin', Brother?"

Rattler handed me a tumbler of whiskey and I could smell the cinnamon from afar. I lifted the glass and took a long swig of the drink. I stared down at the amber liquid for a long minute before I responded.

"Let's just say, I've seen better days."

"We heard about what happened to your girl back then. Sweet thing. We just want you to know, we didn't believe that shit. I've known you my whole life, kid. I respected your father and any decision he made. Just know, not all of us agreed with what was going on."

"I appreciate that. It's good to have friends in low places."

F.O.C.U.S. smirked and took another draw of his cigar. The cloud of smoke hovered around his hard features. "We heard Rancid was down. It's where he belongs."

"No. He belongs on his knees in front of me, begging for his life. I'm just biding my time at this point."

"You planning to get him out?"

"It's what a good brother would do, right?" I looked over at him, an unspoken understanding between us.

"What are you gonna do with him?" Crucifix asked and I smirked.

"Crucify him."

Rattler shook his head. "He has no idea what's comin' for him, but I'm in. Anything you need, you just ask."

Crucifix nodded. "We got your six."

"Appreciate that, Brother. It's good to know not everyone is full of enemy fire."

"When you headin' out?" F.O.C.U.S. took another drag of his cigar and leaned back, propping his foot on his knee.

"I got Knuckles gettin' out in two days, so I gotta leave first thing. Need to run a few errands before I get out there."

"How the fuck did you get Taron Brown out?"

"It's good to have friends in high places too."

One, in particular, was Wolf Stone back in Los Angeles. He was the President of the Hellbound Lovers MC. Three-piece patches who were there when you fucking needed a brother. I'd stopped in a time or two when I needed help. The last time I saw them was right before I took a plane to the end of the world. The Hellbound Lovers had a club called Ravenous in the outskirts of L.A. and it was well known to be neutral grounds. A place where the worst of the worst could seek solace at peace, and I needed their protection. They'd taken me in and offered me a safe roof over my head. Wolf had offered his help at the time, but I never took it. Not until now. His man, Riggs could hack into any system, and Diesel, one of his Enforcers, had connections to the FBI which I needed. All I did was let him know what was going down, and he got me the information I was looking for. It was a favor I'd gladly pay back if they ever needed the Royal Bastards help.

"Turns out our Judge Kempton has some serious skeletons in his closet." I reached into my bag and took out a few shots of the Judge with none other than the Attorney Secretary's granddaughter in a hotel room. "Turns out, he's been fucking her for a couple years now, she just turned eighteen this past month."

"You have to be fucking kidding me," Rattler stared at the pic and raised a brow.

"Turns out the Judge has got one helluva secret. I wonder what his wife and children would think if we plastered his pedophile ass all over social media?"

"Well, I'll be damned. He's one kinky motherfucker too." F.O.C.U.S. chuckled and handed the pic to Crucifix.

"That right there has already been mailed to him anonymously, with one simple demand and a promise that there was more to come. Judge Kempton is going to be one hell of an asset for us, and Knuckles will be out by mid-week."

"You've got some brass ones, brother."

"No. I just know how to play the game. Besides, I ain't goin' down there by myself. There's no way in hell. Knuckles took the fall for something he didn't do. If justice ain't gonna do right by him, I will."

"I don't blame you," F.O.C.U.S. let out a puff of smoke and stared at me. "Not everyone there is on your side. Colt took a chance calling you."

"Why?"

"Because he put his life in your hands. That's some kind of crazy shit, right there."

I stared down at the liquid in my glass, watching it move from side to side. F.O.C.U.S. wasn't wrong. Why Colt would call me knowing I'd skin him alive, was beyond me. Least I could do was hear him out before putting a bullet in his skull.

"Well, either way, it's good to have you back, Jameson."

"I can't say it's good to be back, but it's definitely good to have a drink with old friends."

"Damn straight," F.O.C.U.S. raised his glass and we all took a shot of the whiskey.

"You think I can crash here tonight?"

"Back champagne room is all yours. I'll send you a treat." He signaled to one of the girls who stood behind them, but the one who had her eye on me pushed past the girl he chose and came at me, a sensual easy prowl in her walk. She was gorgeous. Body built for sin, long dark brown hair, and the deepest set of wolf-like eyes I'd ever seen. She had her eyes fixed on F.O.C.U.S. as she grabbed my hand.

He instantly reached out and grabbed her arm. "What do you think you're doing, Nixx?"

"My job."

"I didn't call for you."

"No need to call me, Baby. Besides, I'm just doin' my job."

F.O.C.U.S' jaw locked and I could sense him biting back a retort while she stared back at him almost amused by his reaction. The tension between them was intense, but she never backed down. Feisty little thing.

"Come on, Honey," she turned to me, and slipping out of F.O.C.U.S' grip, she led me through the club and towards one of the back rooms. I didn't ask questions, I just followed her fine ass out the door.

She shoved me down onto a leather couch and I leaned back, getting comfortable as I took a swig of the remaining cinnamon whiskey they'd offered. The music began to play a slow sensual beat and Nixx began to sway to the rhythm.

I followed the pattern of her hips as she moved, her long toned legs slid down the pole, flipping over and opening her thighs giving me a full view of her secrets.

She was beautiful, but as she began to dance and move in front of me my thoughts went to the innocent girl I once knew. I remembered how her auburn locks had specks of gold that would shine in the sunlight. How beautifully innocent she was. Her smile, her bright brown eyes, the way she'd sighed my name when I made love to her.

Nixx ran her hands up my thighs and turned, her perfect

round ass swirling against my semi-hard cock. I took another sip of the whiskey and focused on her hair. How it curled at the ends just like my girl's had. In my haze, I spoke her name and Nixx turned to me and smiled.

"I'll be anyone you want me to be, baby."

I looked into those wolfish gray eyes. This wasn't her. She was gone. She'd been gone for years. Anger started to coil through me and I slowly remembered why the fuck I was here.

"I'm good," I stated as she tried to kiss me while still grinding her pussy against me. She was a needy little thing and any other night I'd be all in, but not tonight.

I turned my head and she pouted. "What? You like to play rough?"

She nipped at my earlobe and whispered huskily. "I can play as rough as you want."

"I said. I'm good." I shoved her off my lap and she landed on her ass. Looking up at me, narrowing her blue-gray eyes.

"F.O.C.U.S. will hear about this."

"You go on and tell him. He'll be pleased to know I didn't fuck the help. Especially when it belongs to him. Now get the fuck out."

She looked mad as hell, yet still beautiful as she cursed the fuck out of me as the door slammed shut behind her sweet ass. I took the last shot of whiskey and raised my legs onto the couch. I stared up at the ceiling and gazed over at a chandelier that hung above my head. The last good memory I had of Willow Braxton was the night before her death, when she kissed me goodbye and I promised her I'd be back. I had never let her down, not until that night. I didn't come home on time. I'd been dragged into a job, and detained under false pretenses. I didn't go through with my promise to come back to her. And it was the biggest mistake I ever made in my life. There wasn't a day I didn't regret it.

Lifting a hand over my head, I closed my eyes. I'd have

another restless night tonight, and a long journey home tomorrow. Getting Knuckles out was easy, getting us back without getting killed, now that was going to be a little harder. I didn't know who was on my side and who wasn't, so I constantly needed to watch our backs. If only I could trust Colt. And if what Crucifix said was true, then Colt was a dead man walking.

2

JAMESON

I LEANED BACK UP against the black Challenger I'd acquired that morning and crossed my arms over my chest as I stared up at the ominous building. He would be walking out at any minute and I wanted to make sure I was here waiting on him. It had been a long time since we'd last seen each other and when I made a promise, I came through with that promise.

The gates opened and as soon as he saw me, he came to me. I was prepared for anything except for what I got. A huge engulfing bear hug.

"Would you get off me?"

He chuckled and backed off, patting my shoulder. "Fuck! It's good to see you!"

Taron Brown was known as Knuckles, brass knuckles which he kept in his back pocket and wielded them when needed. Powerful punches that had put down some mean lookin' motherfuckers. He used to be my Enforcer, falling under Ian Braxton, my appointed Sargent At Arms. I found out from F.O.C.U.S. that Ian went by a different name now. While I sought refuge in Hong Kong. Rael played havoc with the devil and became the Sargent At Arms of the Royal Bastards Nevada Chapter over in

Tonopah Valley. I nearly followed in his footsteps but I'm glad I left. There was some dark fucked up shit immersed in that Chapter. The devil calling out to you on those lonely desert roads. The initiation into Tonopah Valley involved what they called the Devil's Ride, one where you gave your soul away to the devil, and I'm sorry, but I wanted my soul intact. I was already going to hell, and it would not be on some spiritual contract, that shit would be on my own terms.

It was no wonder that the devil called out to me back then. If it weren't for Poe who'd gotten to me and helped me get into Hong Kong, I would probably be ridin' alongside Rael at this moment, and God knows what would have happened to me. I had lost all contact with him, all I knew of him was what F.O.C.U.S. had informed me which was that he took on the fucking name of the archangel of death. He was clearly more fucked up than I thought he was. I'd eventually have to contact him, but I wasn't ready to just yet.

After what Rancid did to his family, Ian had been searching out his own vengeance for years. Didn't surprise me to hear he'd been patched in. He would go to any lengths in order to get his retribution, even if it meant suffering eternal hell. I no longer had him by my side, but I wasn't going in alone. Knuckles was a strong man to have at my back. Retired Special Forces, silent but deadly motherfucker. He usually kept to himself because all in all, I don't even think he trusted himself to be around anyone. But he was loyal to me and I needed that right now. I needed someone I could trust. I wasn't returning without my backup, that was for damn sure.

I signaled for us to get in the car and as soon as we were on the road, he started asking his questions.

"How the hell did you manage to get me the fuck out?"

"I have my connections."

"That is one helluva connection."

"You didn't belong in there anyway."

"Says, who?"

I stared straight ahead, but I could feel his eyes on me. He wasn't wrong. Taron Brown seemed to have his shit together, but in truth, he was a haunted soul. One with a murderous streak and a penchant for pain. He was not the type of man you wanted to have on your bad side. He had no remorse, no guilt, and absolutely no empathy when it came to those who did him wrong. Taron Brown was not one you want to cross, and that was exactly why I needed him.

"You ready to be my Sargent At Arms?"

He looked over at me, his brows furrowing. "They already have a..."

I gave him a grim look and he nodded in understanding. "Thank you, Prez."

I focused on the open road and knew this was not going to be an easy welcome. The Royal Bastards used to be my home, now I was entering into enemy territory. I was brought up with the Royal Bastards. They were my uncles, my brothers, my friends. My father, Paul Jameson-or Bulldog as he was always referred to- was co-founder and President, along with Leo Winters, the Guardian, and Holt Perry, better known as Saddle. They'd given me the opportunity to take over and my father was the first to say he believed I could do this. He always told me how proud he was of me, and although he'd been hard on me, I knew it was because he needed me to be on point.

I'd fought hard to get where I was, to gain the respect of the members. I needed to show I was capable of carrying the torch. That I was able to do the dirt as much as they could, and for years I proved just that. I went up the ranks quickly. From Prospect to Enforcer, to Sargent At Arms. When my father announced he was retiring, he threw my name out there and every single hand went up. Unanimously voted in as the RBMC's National Chapter President. He was so damn proud of me, and I promised I'd live up to his word. But there was always bad shit happening in the shadows. Things none of us were aware of, and when my father died, all that bad shit came to light.

Rancid had been whispering in members' ears for years about how I was going to betray everyone. How I was going to snap. I was the Sargent At Arms when I first encountered Rancid's ruthlessness. I nearly stripped him of his colors and sent him on his way for trying to rape one of the girls who worked the bar. He could have easily taken a club whore, but no, he wanted what he couldn't have.

After talking it out with the executive members we decided that Rancid was an asset. He had a lot of connections and a lot of money, things we needed in order for our name to stay out of law enforcement's ears. But no matter how many connections he might have had, he still needed to be taught a lesson. So I made him into an example. I ordered the members to give him a beating. They brought him down so hard, Ian had to put a stop to it before they killed him. He was then taken to the ER where we later found out he had three broken ribs, a broken arm, a busted jaw, a broken nose, and God knows what else. But he deserved it, and I held no remorse for that. He's lucky they didn't leave him to me. I would have cut his dick off and left him a fucking eunuch.

Now that I think of it, I should have.

What he did in return, was something I would never forget.

Willow had been innocent in all this. Ian was his sister's protector, and when he gave her to me, I swore the same. She meant everything to us. And to see her there. In that way. Her beautiful face marred, unrecognizable. What he did to her deserved no forgiveness.

As I drove down the familiar streets of New Orleans, memories flooded through me. That night, I had been sworn in as President of the National Chapter, but before I could even celebrate, Rancid reached out to let me know we had some dealings we needed to take care of with the Bloody Scorpions. They had stolen some supplies and we needed to get them back. The mission was supposed to be a simple one, but Colt was given another order, and so was Ian. His order to Colt was meant to delay me as much as possible, and he'd started an unnecessary fight with the Blood Scorpions for Rancid. Ian was called on another job clear across town, where he nearly got killed.

When I finally got home, I'd been exhausted. The whole night weighed down on me, and all I really wanted was to get home to see my girl. Instead, what I found was devastation. I'd never felt pain like I did that night. Piercing, agonizing pain that tore at my heart and sucked the life out of me. Elrik Jameson had died that night. I can assure you of that. Knuckles was the one who had found me two days later, lying on the floor by her bedside. He'd dragged me back to the clubhouse, away from the body, thinking he was doing me some good. But he wasn't aware of Rancid's plans and when I arrived, Rancid was ready to take over.

Before we could even bury her, we were blamed. I was accused of raping and murdering the woman I loved, and Ian, for protecting me, went down with me. Before anyone could say otherwise, Rancid was shouting lies, but I was too shocked to even defend myself. The darkness clouded over me and I didn't care about anything anymore. He'd placed a gun to my forehead and forced me my knees. No one spoke up that night. No one stood up to him. They were just as in shock as I was. I remembered some of them shaking their heads. They found it hard to believe, but they had all been psyched into seeing the picture that Rancid was painting.

My patch which I wore as a tattoo, was burned off my skin with a welding torch, stating it was a reprimand for bringing shame onto the Royal Bastards. There was no trial, no jury, just Rancid's orders and everyone followed suit.

"Leave. And don't ever return unless you want me to end your life."

The order was given and I could have left it at that but right away, I knew in my gut what he had done. I knew it was him by the look of satisfaction that reflected on his features. And when I took out my gun to shoot him in the face, fifty other guns were trained on me. I looked around me, at the men who'd called themselves my brothers for so long. The ones who vowed to respect and follow me, those same men were now against me. As soon as I let my guard down, I'd been attacked in the same way I'd done to Rancid years before. I knew then what he wanted.

An eye for an eye.

He laughed as I lay broken and bloodied on the ground. I'd fought as much as I could, but you don't fight against your brothers. You take your beating, for it's supposed to be a lesson taught and received. But there was no lesson there. Just betrayal. Ian was the one who saved me. Soon as he walked in, he pulled the trigger. The bullet had shot right through Rancid's shoulder, bringing him down for only a second before he unleashed everything onto us. The brothers we once had, were firing at us as if we were their enemies. Ian managed to get us both out and we hid out in my father's fishing cabin. As the hours went by we came to the realization that we had to leave. We couldn't do anything for now. We had no weapons, no manpower, and nobody believed us.

That same night, we returned to the clubhouse. We'd taken the gas tanks we left behind the shed and poured gasoline around the grounds, then with no hesitation, we lit the place on fire. It was my father's place. I'd place I'd grown up in. And if I couldn't live there, no one would.

I heard later it was burnt to the ground, while Rancid had been inside. Unfortunately, the asshole must have nine lives, because he'd gotten out and later, I'd heard he'd been reinstated as the National Chapter President. A title that didn't belong to him. One that was stolen with lies and murder. I vowed that day he would pay for what he did. My sole purpose in this life was to do just that. He'd taken everything from me and hurt one of the sweetest most innocent souls. My rage fueled me as I thought about how lonely she must have felt during those last few moments. How absolutely defenseless as he brutalized her.

I gripped the steering wheel as I pumped the gas, taking off.

I was going to rip Rancid apart limb by fucking limb.

3

JAMESON

IT WAS STORMING, and the heavy downpour gave poor visibility as we made our drive down old roads that headed into the backwoods of the Louisiana Bayou. Two hours later we were driving along a dirt road lined with large Spanish Moss that hung low and hid the house from view. We pulled up to a large fence and waited until a man appeared. I didn't recognize the man, but he looked like a mean fucker. Black eyes fixed on the car, black beard that concealed half his features. He was covered in ink and wore just a vest, the Royal Bastards patch emblazoned on it. He stood out in the rain like a dark shadow, waiting.

He came up to the car and I rolled the window down for him. "State your business."

I smirked, ready to give him a smart ass reply, but Knuckles intervened. "Let us through, Riddick. We didn't come here to make small talk with you."

He grimaced and squinted at him, and he nodded slowly as his eyes shifted between us.

"How the fuck did you get out?"

"See, now you know that's none of your business, Riddick."

24

"I ain't lettin' delinquents in here."

I narrowed my eyes on him starting to get aggravated by all the bullshit he was spewing. The guy was huge, but I was pretty sure if he kept that shit up I was gonna reach out and slam his head into my dashboard.

"Just open the damn gate and let your VP know Elrik Jameson has arrived."

The guy took a step back, and in one swift move, he removed the chain and popped open the gate. "I apologize, Prez. I didn't know who you were."

I turned in my seat and looked him dead in the eye. "Riddick, right?"

"Yes, Sir."

"Just stay the fuck out of my way and I may spare your life."

"Yes, Sir."

I looked over at Knuckles who rolled his eyes at me. As we drove past Riddick slowly I got the lowdown on him. "What does he do around here?"

"Enforcer."

"Is he one to trust?"

"Yeah. I'd say so. He doesn't know you and goes along with whatever Colt decides. He's loyal to the VP, he was the one who brought him in."

I gripped the wheel as the huge two-story house came into view. It was located right along the river.

There were several bikes parked beneath the first floor. Two large shacks stood on the right. Behind them, a long winding path that led to nowhere. An old well stood off to the side and from where we stood we could see there was a boat shed further along the water. An airboat and two smaller motorboats stood beneath it.

We stared up at the house and Knuckles whistled. "You see that up there?"

I followed his eyesight and right above the house's attic was what seemed like a lookout. It was located smack center on the roof of the house.

"Looks like an old church."

"You never know with these old buildings out here. You know what they say."

"What's that?"

"All roads lead to Rome."

"This ain't Rome, Brother. This right here is purgatory."

As we walked up to the front of the house, Colton Winters stepped out. He had two other men with him, one I recognized as Styx, one of our older Enforcers. He nodded to Knuckles who made his quiet stance by my side. Making it clear as day whose side he was on.

"Colt."

"Jameson." His eyes looked warily from Knuckles then back to me, probably wondering if this was a good idea, or even if I'd leave him with his life intact.

Colt had been a very good friend of mine, at one time. We'd grown up together, with Ian. His father and my father were close. Leo Winters now lived a few miles away with his wife, December. He'd always been family to me, loyal as fuck, too bad his son was questionable.

"You mind telling me why the fuck I'm here."

"Didn't expect you to bring backup."

"Did you think I was stupid."

"Never said that."

"No, you just implied it. That's all you need to judge a man anyway, don't you Colt?"

His eyes held mine in a steady all-knowing gaze. I was full of anger, and his expression told me he was doubting all this.

Too bad motherfucker. You called me here for a reason and I ain't going back.

We never did have to speak out loud to know what each of us was thinking. The tension in the air was thick. It wasn't until

December Winters walked out from behind her son, with a big smile on her face, that the tension broke.

"Elrik! Oh my God!" She ran up to me and right into my arms. It was so damn good to see her. I immediately let go of my apprehensions and hugged her tight. She was a breath of fresh air amid all this built-up tension.

"Hi, Momma."

"My God, you've gotten old." She laughed and cradled my cheeks.

"And you look as beautiful as ever."

"With all these grays?" She smiled at me tenderly. "It's so good to have you back."

"It's good to see you too, Momma."

She smiled with tears in her eyes. "Stupid fools taking you away from me." She hugged me tight and for the first time in three years, I could feel emotions trickling in. Emotions I'd buried deep down, and I didn't like them one bit.

December Winters had been the only motherly figure in my life. She took care of me when I was growing up and made sure Bulldog was giving me a decent upbringing. My real mother had been taken from us. She was diagnosed with cervical cancer and she passed when I was four years old. I had seen a picture of her once, but my father never spoke of her. December reminded me of her, her lavender scent, her kind smile, there was something familiar there. She took care of me when my father had to go on runs, and Colt and I, with his sister Stephanie, grew up together. It had been all good, at one point in time. That was until her son betrayed me.

"Where's Leo?"

"Out and about, had some errands to run. He'll come see you later. I made you boys a big dinner. I'm sure you've been traveling all over. Come on in, honey."

I let her lead me into the house. A large staircase stood in the center of the home, leading up to the rooms upstairs and it split the large house in two. To the left was what looked like a bar with its own entrance off to the side. To the right was the actual home. I was led towards the bar.

Stepping in through the doorway, the space was narrow. Bar stools stood along a long cherry wood counter, small tables across from it. A small stage at the entrance.

"Welcome to the Battering Hole."

"You call this a bar?"

"It's only for the members. We hold Church here. We'll be holding it tonight."

I eyed him, but he avoided my gaze. He knew I wasn't prepared for all this. The last thing I wanted was to have Church tonight.

"I'm not going."

"It's mandatory." He stated, his anger now coming through.

"I ain't one of you, or did you forget."

Heavy silence hovered over us and I could tell that it had become awkward for December. "Momma. I appreciate everything you're doing but...."

She raised her hands and nodded. "No need to say anything. I understand."

Going over to her son, she cradled his cheeks and brought him down to her, kissing him on the forehead. She whispered something to him before coming up to me and doing the same, only the words she whispered, were a Mother's plea.

"Please don't take my son away from me."

I stared down at her, tears filled her eyes and my heart broke.

"Hear him out first, Elrik." She stroked my cheek and with a broken smile for me, she left us alone.

I stared at the closed door for a long moment, and then I turned to Knuckles. "Leave us."

Colt nodded to Styx and signaled for him to do the same. We waited quietly as they left, finally leaving us alone.

"Do you want to know why I haven't put a bullet in your skull?" I spoke without looking back at him.

"No."

"Because of that woman," I pointed at the closed door from where December had disappeared through. I looked back at him, allowing him to see my anger.

"She's the only reason. When she dies. You'll soon follow."

"Elrik."

I held my hand up because I was done listening to them. I was done not having a voice in all this. "You called me back thinking...what? I'd take pity on your soul. Motherfucker, you have no idea what kind of wrath I'm going to bring down on you."

"I understand you believe I did you wrong."

"Did me wrong?" I turned to him. "You took everything from me!" I roared into the silence and the words echoed around us.

"You helped him ruin my life," I walked up to him, my finger shaking at him as I tried to control myself. "And you will pay for what you did, and for the life you helped destroy."

He hung his head and it took him a second for him to reply. "I probably deserve that."

I gritted my teeth and clenched my fists. How dare he act the martyr, as if this wasn't at all his fault. He followed directives, made calls, set it all up so that I would fail to come home. I was detained because of him, and because of that, the most important person in my life was destroyed. He went against me and broke code at every turn. What the fuck made him think I'd ever want him by my side again.

"We'll start with stripping away your title," my tone held a sharp edge to it that made him take a step back.

"Don't worry," I patted his arm, right where I knew his tattoo was etched. "I won't torch it away. At best, I'll filet the fuck out of it."

Turning, I walked towards the entrance. "Cancel the fucking meeting. We have Church when I say we have Church!"

I slammed the door behind me and headed out towards the car. Knuckles was waiting for me out there and as I stepped down from the front porch, Styx eyed me.

"You better watch those eyes boy, unless you want them carved from your head."

He instantly looked down and I smirked. At least there was some respect still left.

"What happened?" Knuckles spread his arms, as I went down the steps and towards the car.

"We're not staying here."

"We're not?" He followed me into the car and as I started the ignition, Colt came out to the porch. He stared at me as I revved the car up and slid it out of the grounds. The wheels skidded out as I turned, sending mud flying their way.

"I'm not staying anywhere until I know I'm surrounded by people I trust."

He smirked. "So where are we going?"

"Home."

A half an hour later, we pulled up to the old cabin that was stationed out a few miles from the old clubhouse. It was my father's place, and I had been the only one who knew about it until a few weeks ago when I lent it to F.O.C.U.S. to use as a safe house. My father and I would come out here fishing, or to have a beer. It was our place. A space away from all the shit the MC drove in. Hidden in the woods, it was the perfect hideout and place to lay our heads for a few nights until I decided what the fuck I was going to do with Colt and the rest of those men.

After settling in and having something to eat, we both sat by the fire in silence, each holding a whiskey glass and a somber expression.

Taking a sip, Knuckles sighed and eyed the glass. "Fuck, it's been a long time since I had a good drink."

Knuckles had been a heavy drinker at one point. He used liquor to forget his past. I never did want to know what kind of demons waited for him at night, but I knew they still haunted him.

"I thought you quit?"

"So did I," he stared at it long and hard before chugging down the rest of it.

"You wanna tell me what is going on in that head of yours?"

"I don't even know half the time."

"We're gonna get killed out here," he whispered.

"I've got way too much shit to plan before I let myself get killed by some mediocre assholes."

"So what is your plan?"

I stared down at the glass and smiled. "I'mma let 'em sweat a little. And when I do come back, there will be changes made and heads to cut."

"Just like that?"

I nodded. "Just. Like. That."

"They're not gonna take that lightly. You've got to expect a fight."

"I don't expect anything less. What I do need is the roll call sheet. You think you can get that for me?"

"You got it, Prez."

"I need to know exactly who is still here and if there are any new members, who brought them in. We need to know what can be recycled, and what needs to be trashed."

"I'm on it."

"Do you know anything about the house?"

Knuckles shrugged. "All I know is that when shit went down, your father's clubhouse burnt down. Rancid acquired the house right after I was sent to jail. Word is he got it from the insurance money."

I stared at him. There shouldn't have been any insurance money. It all belonged to me. "I wasn't here to sign off on that."

Knuckles looked down at the ground. "You may want to ask Forger, then."

Forger was the Treasurer of the club. He dealt with all the paperwork, he was accountable for the money intake, and all offshore accounts. He was the one who signed off on deals and made sure our money was divvied up evenly among us. He was also in charge of the estate and everything that went with it.

I was going to kill the motherfucker for stealing what was rightfully mine.

"It's a pretty large property. I think it's got like eighteen acres of hunting ground all around and of course, it's on the Bayou. Overall it was a decent investment."

I stayed quiet, contemplating how the fuck I was going to make Rancid pay for all this. I could sense Knuckles wanted to say something.

"Just ask the fucking question."

"What are you gonna do with Colt?"

"First Church meeting comes to order, he's stripped of his title. He ain't no VP to Elrik Jameson. What he is is a traitorous bastard who will get beat down to within a second of his life."

"He's gone through a lot, Prez. I was here, I saw how it all went down. How much he took to the bottle after you and Ian left. I think he was being sincere. Besides, the last time someone went against Rancid, shit changed and everybody understood that it was their life they were putting on the line. No one wants to die, Brother."

"What happened last time?"

"He killed off Dog.""Are you fucking kidding me." Dog was the President of the Baltimore Chapter. From what I could remember, he always respected my father, and in turn, he respected me. He was more than eager to vote me in as Prez.

"I wish I was. He wanted to overthrow Rancid and somehow he found out about it. I think it was one of the club whores who snitched. He brought in Gamble and did a number on the poor girl. Raped her as he saw fit and put a baby in her belly."

"She's pregnant?"

"'Bout due, I think."

I recalled Gamble, she was a pretty little blonde. By the time I met her she was around nineteen, and Rancid didn't let her out of his sight. I didn't know why she'd arrived with him, just figured she was his Old Lady. Back then I was too involved in doing my own thing, and never really directed my focus on her. Besides, I was told never to go near her by my father, and I followed orders.

It wasn't until later I found out Rancid had selected her as his own personal whore. It was degrading what he'd done to her at such a young age, and how he ruined her family and her father. He was pillaging clubs even before he snuck into the New Orleans Chapter. I should have known he was biding his time. He'd sweet-talked my father, been the exemplary Lead Enforcer after Leo Winters left. I didn't know why the fuck my father kept that motherfucker around. He always did tell me to keep my enemies close. I just didn't know how close they actually were.

"He named her President of the Baltimore Chapter."

"He did what?!"

"Wanted to humiliate her, I guess. He made her Royal Bastards property and any club President could use her as their whore. I'm pretty sure Heavy indulged in that, but so did Rancid. That motherfucker brutalized her and then threw her to the wolves, who turned out they were pretty damn loyal to her."

I nodded. "Which is why I believe what Colt is doing deserved some respect. He's putting his life on the line for you."

"I don't trust him."

"I think you should give him the benefit of the doubt."

"And I think you have no fucking say in my business," I growled, shifting my eyes on him.

He nodded and stood up. " You're right. You do what you need to do. I'mma go shower. Get to bed. It's been a long trip. I think you should do the same. I'll get you what you need, first thing."

He walked out leaving me to my own murderous thoughts. My eyes followed the flicks of the flames and the more I thought about it, the more I considered Rancid a cancerous fuck. He'd not only managed to steal what rightfully belonged to me, but he went around killing brothers left and right. The fucker was going to suffer. I guaranteed that.

❦ 4 ❦

JAMESON

A WEEK LATER...

I WALKED INTO THE HOUSE FOR THE FIRST TIME SINCE I ARRIVED. Styx was leaning up against the bar and a few other members were mulling around. Some acknowledged me when I arrived, others completely ignored my presence. That would change, very soon. They had no fucking clue who I was.

Styx signaled to me and we moved over to a private section of the bar.

"You got a present waiting for ya." Styx nodded towards the back door.

I narrowed my eyes on him, still not trusting half the fuckers in here. "What kind of present?"

"It's out back."

He stood there staring at me, and I swept my hand out and widened my eyes. "Well, lead the fucking way."

He grunted but kept his mouth shut as he led the way out back. I followed him past the metal shacks and towards that path I'd seen earlier. The one that led to nowhere. I stopped in my tracks. "What the fuck is that?"

"Look, Prez, I'm not here to break your balls. I was tasked with the job to protect you so you can either trust me, or kick me the fuck out, but I ain't playin' games here."

I stared at him and nodded. "That's fair enough."

He continued to walk down the path and I followed him, looking behind me as we hiked. I wasn't expecting any surprises, but I also wasn't going to let my guard down either way. I figured I'd get to know Styx since he was put in charge of protecting me and all.

"How'd you become a Royal Bastard?"

"I had just gotten out of the military, and I got into a bar fight with the Bloody Scorpions. Colt saw it and decided to bring me in. Haven't looked back since."

I whistled. "Lucky you didn't get yourself killed."

"Those fuckers had no chance. I was on edge that night, my sister had wanted to take me out to dinner, put two of them down for thinking they could lay a hand on her. You don't fuck with my family unless you want to get killed. And those fuckers were clearly lookin' for a world of hurt that night."

As we talked it turned out, I realized I didn't disapprove of Styx. At least I liked the way he processed shit. No one fucked with family. That's the one thing that I considered club code. Loyalty is King and the MC is your family. Let's see how many of these assholes were actually willing to put their neck on the line for their new Prez. Styx was high on my trust list at the moment. Knuckles had informed me earlier that he was used as a sort of bounty hunter. As the Enforcer for Rancid, he went around collecting debts as well as bodies. If someone didn't pay up, you'd call Styx. He didn't give you an ultimatum. He was the one you needed to pay to live, if not he'd send you straight to hell. He had no remorse, no morals, cold as they come.

"You're an Enforcer then?"

"Yes, Sir, I am."

"Good. You mind workin' with Knuckles."

"I don't see a problem with it. That motherfucker is crazy but I'd rather have him on my side than on enemy lines."

I nodded in agreement. The chatting stopped as we came to a large metal barn. "What the fuck is this?"

"We found it a few weeks after Rancid got locked up. It was off-limits to everyone, we now know why. This was his private quarters."

"Interesting."

"You haven't seen the half of it. Just wait."

He unlocked the chains that held the doors secure. Inside was pitch black until he flipped the switch and lit up the dingy space in a pale, almost bluish light. In the center of the room was a large empty cell. A cot lay at the far corner, and on it lay a woman. I looked over at Styx and he shrugged. Surrounding the cell, there was everything from leather straps and crops of all sizes, to large saws and steel hand sickles that swung from the ceiling on one end of the barn. I stood there for a second, almost feeling giddy. Fucker had his very own torture room.

"Has the FBI seen this?"

"Not that I know of."

My eyes traveled along the sharp edges of one of the blades. "Good."

I had a feeling those saws were drenched in the blood of the girls whose lives he took. "No one goes near any of it. I don't want anyone's fingerprints on these."

"What should we do with them?"

"Pack them up for now and keep them out of sight. We'll deal with them later."

My eyes searched the cold interior. The cell was old, the heavy steel bars were peeling, the place dirty and dank. My eyes fell upon the woman.

"Who is she?"

"Sadie Forrester."

The name didn't register. "Who sent her?"

I approached slowly, circling the cage, her blonde locks were splayed in disarray over the pillow, half-covering her pale features. Her plush tits molded to the pillow she was curled into, two soft mounds of flesh I suddenly wanted to get my hands on. Her lips protruded in a delicate pink pout as she slept.

"She's out cold for now. We made sure of that. But it's been a few hours, she may wake up any second now."

"And what the fuck am I supposed to do with her?"

He shrugged. "Do what you do best. She betrayed Petros." I looked up at him, narrowing my eyes. Petros and I never really saw eye to eye, but we respected each other. He was the Nebraska Chapter President, and he was one who loved to test my limits.

I crouched down near her head, studying her. "How did she betray him?"

"Fucked around on him with his VP, Hart."

"Did she really?"

"Says, since you're back, you might as well prove your loyalty. She deserves punishment. He doesn't give a shit what you do to her, so long as she suffers.

"She must have some fine pussy if he wants her tortured. Did a number on him, I suppose?"

"Have no fucking clue."

"Where's Hart?"

"Rancid sent him over to Gamble's Baltimore Chapter."

"And Petros sent her to me?" I was disgusted. He knew damn well the type of vicious shit I could do to her. "What the fuck is he expecting?"

"Loyalty. He's testing you. Word is out, Jameson. He wants you to prove yourself."

"By killing a fucking innocent girl?"

"By showing your loyalty. Mark her, torture her, do what you must, but Petros wants justice done."

I stared back at him. "I'll do with her as I damn well please."

"He wants a confession. The truth of her fucking around with Hart so that Hart can get his punishment. He's pissed that Rancid so easily dismissed him. So don't kill her too quickly before you get it out of her."

He headed up the stairs, the door slamming behind him as he left me alone with her.

"Fuck," I gritted as the woman stirred on the cot. Her hair fell to the side exposing her delicate neckline. Either I'd been without for a while, or this woman was a Lwa, a spirit sent from the heavens to torture me. She was gorgeous. Soft features, high cheekbones, a delicate nose, and those lips. Lips that spoke of sin and lust. She was extremely beautiful and extremely dangerous. What the creole people liked to call bèt seksyèl or a sexual creature. I had this dark ominous feeling, she was going to bring me to Papa Legba's doorstep, and I predicted that for her, I would face the devil.

I shook the thought from my head. Those thoughts only brought death and despair. I didn't want to think about the darkness that surrounded me. There was no room for love in those shadows. I'd been at the crossroads. Face to face with the devil himself. There was no turning back. I had a debt owed, and an act of vengeance to be paid. That was my only focus. It had to be.

She stirred again and suddenly her eyes opened. She gasped when she sensed she wasn't alone, and quickly scurried away, curling up in the corner of the cot. Bright, scared, blue eyes stared back at me. She pressed herself back against the bars of the cell as she stared out into the shadows where I hid.

"Wh-where am I? What is this place?"

"I remained hidden, watching her. I didn't want her to know what my face looked like just yet. It was all psychological. Just make her believe you're hideous causing her anxiety to peak and with it a sleepless night of wondering what was to come next. "You're on Royal Bastards ground."

"Where?"

"Does it matter?"

"What do you want from me?"

"It's not what I want. And just so we're clear I didn't drag you in here."

She looked down at her feet, biting her lip as if she were trying to remember something. "Do you know how you got here?"

"No," she replied, the word barely audible. She was lying.

She looked up at me warily. "I'm not in Lincoln anymore, am I?"

I lit up a cigarette and stood there for a long minute, swirling the smoke around. "No. You are not."

She got up on her knees and grabbed the bars. "Please let me out."

"I can't do that."

"Why?" Her voice trembled and involuntarily my cock twitched at her plea.

"You know why."

"No! I don't know which is why I'm asking you!"

She screamed and sobbed the words out, anger and desperation settling in. "I suggest you calm the fuck down."

"I didn't do anything," she whimpered as tears slid down her cheeks.

"Are you sure about that?"

"Yes," she seethed with conviction, her eyes trying to make out my face and I took a step back, remaining in those shadows.

"Seems like they've put me in a tough spot."

"Why is that?"

"Because you were brought to me so that I can punish you."

I could see her bottom lip tremble. "Seems like you betrayed someone you shouldn't have ever crossed."

"I did not."

"You can continue lying all you want. You're here for a reason, Sadie Forrester. And we'll get the truth out of you sooner or later."

"You're wrong! You're all wrong!"

"We'll see about that."

I made my way towards the door, her pleas following me. Her scream of rage got swallowed up in the darkness as I shut the light and the door slammed behind me.

I paused for a second and smirked. She was ferocious and angry, and I liked that fight in her. I

I made my way down the path, her bright eyes engraved in my head. She looked so lost, so desperate. Innocent face, big eyes, golden locks that silhouetted such pain-stricken features. She was almost haunting to look at. As if her heart had broken and she was fighting to live.

Strolling into the house, I made my way back to the bar where Styx was seated. I grabbed his shot of whiskey and downed it.

"What are you thinkin', Prez?"

"I'm thinking that girl down there. That is one fine piece of ass."

Styx smirked. "Damn straight, she is. But that is one dangerous piece of ass."

"I don't know what Petros wants me to do with her, but I don't kill women."

"Fuck if I know what he wants. To be honest, I don't think he even cares about her that much."

"I wouldn't either if she fucked around on me. But that girl down there doesn't look like the type."

"So what are you gonna do with her?"

"Fuck if I know. She's just another problem that ain't mine.

One who landed on my doorstep without me even asking for it."

"Isn't that always the case around these parts?"

I shrugged. What was I going to do with the woman? I mean, I could do a lot to that voluptuous body of hers. I could ruin her in so many unimaginable ways. I signaled to the bottle and Styx poured me another shot of whiskey. Downing it, I stared at myself in the mirror that spanned the bar across from me. I hated mirrors, I always thought if you stared at them long enough, you could the demons that lurked inside your soul. For a brief moment, I thought I saw them. I was staring at the reflection of a man I no longer recognized. My eyes looked dark and bloodshot, my features grim and menacing, and as I brought the glass up to my lips, I wondered if after all this was said in done, I could ever find the man I once was.

I couldn't live with myself after Willow's death. She'd been just a pawn in a brutal game that was meant to hurt me. And hurt me, it did. It tore the soul from me. I was never the same after that. My depression was so deep I found myself lost in the streets of Hong Kong. Looking for solace in the darkness that I didn't even know existed.

I always felt like the devil was watching every move I made. Like his hand reached out to mine and moved it accordingly. No matter what protection spell I used, or how many times the cards were read to me, the reading was always the same. It would all end in death and a burning inferno of a tower.

I set the glass down, hiding the image of her face. I couldn't bear to look at it. The power of the cards called out to me and quickly, I made my way back to the private office that was set aside. Locking the door, I took out the stack of tarot cards I always carried with me. Spreading them out on the table before me, I asked what I wanted. They always held an answer. This time I asked for guidance.

A three-card spread was laid out before me, and I hesitated

before turning the cards. When I did, the message was as clear as day. I had to do what I had to do. I stroked the Empress card as I stared down at the Ace of Wands and the Ten of Swords. Betrayal, sex, and a woman who personified sex. The Ten of Swords were always in my readings. Maybe my life was centered around just that...betrayal. But at the same time...

I lay the Empress on the table before me and stared down at her. She was going to be my biggest downfall, this I knew beyond a shadow of a doubt.

What the fuck was coming my way?

5

SADIE

I WAS STRAPPED TO A CHAIR. My wrists bound by leather to wooden arms, my legs strapped back, feet curled behind the wooden legs. I rocked back slightly and that's when the rope on my neck and along my diaphragm tightened simultaneously.

I remained still, taking shallow breaths as I was forced in an awkward position. Neck back against the head of the seat, chest arched out just enough to loosen the ties. If I moved again, my breath would be cut off, so I remained still. Unmoving. And I waited.

That's when he stepped out of the shadows and I was caught off guard. He was gorgeous. Dark blonde hair, chiseled features, green eyes, and he wore a sly smirk along his plush lips. He stood there in a black button-down shirt rolled up at the elbows, wearing dark jeans and black boots. His muscles straining along the thin cotton while tattoos outlined his forearms. He wore a black stone on a leather strap around his neck, it looked old and worn. Rings aligned his fingers, some were of skulls and my eyes recognized one that held the Celtic pentagram, a symbol of protection. I had to admit, his sexual prowess was undeniable.

"Wh-who are you?"

"Wrong question."

"You're the same man who was here with me the other day, aren't you?"

He watched me beneath a dark hooded gaze and as he leaned into me his green eyes sparkled. He seemed to be enjoying my discomfort, or maybe it was my naiveness that brought that glean into his eye.

"I heard what you did, Sadie." His fingers tugged on the strap of my tank top, pulling it and snapping it onto my flesh. The act made me jump and I could sense the rope quiver under the faint movement. His eyes lingered along the bare flesh of my breasts and my nipples tightened beneath the cotton.

He shook his head, sliding his fingers across the rope, lightly grazing my neck. "If you move, she'll tighten on you and take your breath away. If she squeezes just enough," he placed his palm around the nape of my neck and squeezed for emphasis. "She may even snap this fragile neck of yours. And we wouldn't want you to die so soon, now would we Sadie."

"You're crazy."

He smiled. "So I've been told."

"Let me go. Please."

"It's not that easy, Sadie. You were sent to me for a reason. You were meant to be here, I'm just not sure yet what for. I haven't quite figured out all the signs. But I will."

"He sent me here, didn't he?" Tears threatened to fall but I refused to let them. Instead, I swallowed them down, not giving any of them that satisfaction.

My feelings remained sealed. He had no right to know any of them, and either way, the pain Petros had caused was enough to drown me in sorrow.

"There's nothing you can do to me that will be more painful than what I've already gone through."

His eyes met mine and I found them to be unnerving.

They were beautiful yet in their depths lay a darkness so deep, and there was so much pain, which reflected my own. He was filled with the same pain and anger that coursed through my veins.

"I beg to differ," he stated, his eyes roaming my face and chest. A finger came out and ran along the soft flesh that protruded along my chest. I shivered and when I shifted back, the ropes tightened and I gasp for air.

"I told you not to move."

"Fuck. You." I gritted as the rope continued to tighten around my neck, restricting my airflow.

"It takes minutes for someone to die when choked. Did you know that?"

I stared back at him, fear now settling deep in my gut. I was given to this man to hurt me. And if I allowed it, he would hurt me.

"Please," the little bit of air I sucked in, allowed me to beg.

"With each shallow breath you take, Sadie, you'll come to the realization of just how important air can be to a person. Five minutes without sufficient air and you are declared brain dead. Not enough inhales to the lungs causes the body to lose control. Involuntarily fighting to live. The more you move, the more she tightens."

My chest ached as I struggled to take in a deeper inhale, restricted by the rope around my torso. "You're an animal," I wheezed.

He smirked. "I'm worse than an animal. I'm Vengeance."

"Why are you doing this to me?"

"I could give a shit about your betrayal. To be honest, I'm just bored."

"He's not worth this."

"You're right," he nodded in agreement. "No one's worth this much desperation, not unless you loved him."

I closed my eyes and concentrated on my breathing. He was

using some fucked up mind games to get to me. "I did nothing wrong."

"My understanding is you had your way with the VP. Hart."

I shifted and the rope tightened once again. I gasped for air and my eyes went wide.

"I told you not to move," his lips were a fraction of an inch from mine. "You move again, and I'll let the rope tighten around that pretty neck of yours until it snaps."

I struggled for breath, but as I leaned back, my chest out, his eyes lingered on me.

"What you're saying is a fabrication of lies," I whispered between small intakes of breath. "They made that all up in their head."

He tsked, sliding his fingers down my cheek, his eyes following the trail. "You wouldn't believe what happens to traitors around here." His dark eyes met mine. "Trust me. I know."

"I'm not a traitor. I... I loved Petros."

The man's eyes narrowed on me and he stared at me for a long minute. "Then why are you here?"

"Because..." I swallowed and at the same time strained for breath. Small shallow breaths that barely reached my lungs. The burning ache in my chest was now more than uncomfortable.

"Because, what?"

I could see that was what he wanted. A confession. But what happened between Hart and me, I'd never tell a soul. What for? What was done was done.

"If you want to kill me... d-do it now," I took in a trembling breath. " I'm-I'm already numb. Just drive th-the blade through my heart." I struggled again for air. "It can't...hurt...any more than it already...does."

He stared at me, and as he did, I let the tears fall. I'd given myself completely to Petros. Every ounce of love I could muster, and in the end, I was just his whore. A cumslut that warmed his bed. It didn't matter how much I loved him. I was never enough.

He'd cared about me so little, that he gave me to the mercy of this man. This stranger who wanted to torture me. I honestly thought a stab to the heart would probably be less painful.

He leaned in and gripped my chin, pressing my head further back, the pressure released on my lungs and I was able to take in a gulp of air, with it the scent of his cologne mixed with leather. He stared down at me, his breaths sweeping against my lips.

"Don't ever think you have the upper hand. I will break you so fast you wouldn't even know what hit you."

He yanked his hand away and the movement made the rope tighten. My eyes went wide as the air was cut off completely, and I stayed suspended at that moment for what seemed like an eternity. The sound of a switchblade echoed in the room, and suddenly the pressure was released. The rope on my neck fell away but it was replaced by his hand. I fought for air and struggled against the ropes, but he squeezed tightly, letting me know there was no escape. As his lips brushed against my ear, a blade shined in his hand and I glanced down as he pointed it to my heart.

"This, right here," he tapped on my flesh, right above my heart, with the tip of the knife. "This is bullshit. It's just there to cause pain and destruction. It's not worth paying any attention to it. If I could, I'd carve it out for you, hand it to you and let you squeeze it until it stops pumping. That's the only way to stop the suffering." The tip of the blade ran along my chest, slicing just above the first layer of skin and a thin crimson line appeared. The sight of it was almost surreal.

"No one ever said love was easy."

He left my side then and simply walked away. I stared at his back, stunned by his words. This man was beyond strange, he harbored deep sorrow and it almost tore all my inhibitions away. He could have easily killed me, but he didn't. Yet I knew he'd be back for me. I knew I was dragged in here to tell the truth.

I wondered where Hart was, if he'd lived after helping me. What we did was unforgivable, and I'd used him. I'd used him because I was jealous, and I was enraged and blinded by it. I didn't ever want to feel that way again. But Petros didn't have the right to get peace of mind. I wanted him to suffer from that doubt. The doubt that he also wasn't good enough.

❧ 6 ❧

JAMESON

FLAMES ENGULFED the clubhouse and the light rustling of the wind ran through the Spanish Moss, their branches swaying back and forth, creating shadows in the moonlight. Willow's face appeared among the flames, screaming for help, and as much as I tried to get to her, I couldn't. Her sobs and pleas echoed around me and a scream of desperation ripped out of me. I felt so fucking helpless, so alone. Covering my face, I sobbed.

Someone placed their hand on my shoulder and when I turned towards them, the flames were gone and in the middle of the room stood Sadie. She looked at me beneath long lashes and gave me a knowing smile. She was dressed in a little white baby doll that barely covered her body. Her lush breasts could be seen through the sheer material, the lace split at the end to give me a view of her thong.

My cock throbbed at the sight of her, the flames and pain now long forgotten. Taking me by the hand she guided me to the bed, lying back on it and luring me in between her legs. I hovered over her, her body undulating beneath me. A true seductress that made me lose my way. I was afraid to touch her, afraid to go near her. And as she sighed my name I knew that if I did, I'd never find my way back to reality.

I fought with myself, my hands hovering over her body, but not touching. She placed my hand over her slick mound and we both moaned as my fingers entered her. Slow movements as I watched her fuck and play with me. This was wrong. So fucking wrong.

And as I closed my eyes I tried to control this lust I was feeling, when I reopened them, Willow stared back at me. A blank look in her eyes. Almost accusatory. I leaped back and as I did the sheets began to soak through in a bright crimson. The blood of the one I loved now marring the dream. And when my eyes fell upon hers, I let out an agonized scream. For I wasn't looking at her anymore, I was looking into the pit of death and it was calling out to me.

My eyes snapped open and I sat up. I was drenched in sweat, my hands were shaking. And as I brought them up to my face, the tears I'd never released while awake, managed to overtake me in my dreams. I hadn't had nightmares like these in years and I fucking hated them. I knew returning was a bad idea. I knew they would return.

When I first arrived in Hong Kong, I had nowhere to go. I was so lost in my depression, I just lived out in the streets, eating whatever scraps of food I could find. An old man approached me one afternoon. He didn't speak much English, but he managed to tell me that he practiced Buddhism and he saw something in me that called out to him. He took me in, taught me what it meant to live in a place like Hong Kong, and helped me find peace in meditation. He'd told me the nightmares never truly went away, but if I searched within myself, I could release them. Eventually, I learned once again to sleep, and with that sleep came healing. He died a few years ago. He'd been my only friend back in Hong Kong. The only one I trusted. But he taught me a valuable lesson and taught me that no good came from evil. I held onto that one good thing he imposed on me. I took it with me wherever I went.

Getting up, I walked over to the bathroom, squinting as I turned on the light. I looked up at myself in the mirror. The man staring back at me was a dark shadow. Blackened soul and weary-eyed. I leaned down and splashed water on my face then shut the light and slowly crawled back into bed.

My thoughts veered off to the blonde locked up in a cell down that lonely path. She must be cold, afraid, alone. I had felt that unnerving sense of doom before, and I knew it had to play havoc on her nerves. I shouldn't be thinking of her, she was an unwanted distraction, yet there was just something about the woman that held me captivated. So soft, yet fierce. She wouldn't go down without a fight and I wondered how it would feel to have her nails scratch at my back, her wails of agonized pleasure being stolen by my kiss as I fucked her hard and rough.

My hand traveled down to my cock, and the image of her in that white silk piece only made me groan in need. I hadn't had a woman since my Willow died. I didn't really feel the need for one. In Hong Kong, there were prostitutes at every corner, a dime a dozen, and I satisfied my needs with them. But in all these years, no one held my attention as Sadie Forrester did.

She was a pain slut, I could tell by the way she trembled at my touch. I tugged on my dick as I pictured her in that damn white number, bent on all fours and showing me her heart-shaped ass. Offering it to me as her fingers traced her swollen pussy lips. My hips lifted as I pictured my handprints on her flesh. The sound of a crop sweeping down and that sweet cry she'd give out as I inflicted that pain onto her. Filling her perfect unmarred flesh with fine red welts that she'd feel for days.

She flicked her clit as she spiraled into an orgasm from the dark games I imposed on her body. Causing me to moan, as in my head I finally entered her slick mound. Sliding in deep and holding her there, perched on my cock, as my heartbeat pulsed inside of her. Finally claiming what I wanted. The urge to inflict pain on her matched the craving I had to give her pleasure. I wanted her coming undone on my cock. And I stroked myself to the rhythm of her sexual movements, movements that in my mind, had her needing me just as badly. As she turned her head to look at me I roared out my release. Those bright blue eyes spoke of a lust that was only rivaled by my own primal needs. Her cries of my name, how I wanted to hear my name on her lips, as I drove myself into her tight wetness. The mere thought of it had me grunting as I jerked off for her.

"Sadie, fuck," I moaned as I exploded. Shaking as in my fantasies she received every drop of my cum on her tongue. Licking me all up before thanking me.

"Fuck!" I threw my head back into the pillows, rubbing my forehead, my other hand letting my cock fall limp.

I turned my head towards the window. The sun had begun to rise and streaks of pink hues were starting to appear in the sky. Traces of blue peaked from behind white clouds, and her eyes came to mind once again. She was hiding things and for some reason, that bothered me. I wanted to know everything about her.

Where she came from.

What her childhood was like.

How much pain could she endure at my hands, before I sent her over the edge of pleasure?

I could give a shit about Petros and his punishments. I wasn't going to give him that satisfaction. But I would get the truth out of her, for me. I needed to know. It had somehow become an obsession for me. I wanted to know what this woman had done to make Petros abhor her as he did, and why did she do it.

Is she truly as disloyal as they all made her out to be?

If there was one thing the Royal Bastards lived by, it was loyalty and code. She'd broken that for Petros. She'd betrayed him by warming another man's bed. But the question wasn't if she did it, the question was if she loved him as much as she said she did, then why did she do it. There was so much more to this woman. Layers upon layers I wanted to peel away. No one had ever made me feel compassion like she did. The need for it was etched in her heart. The need to be loved.

Love.

Such a foolish, perverse notion.

It fucking raped you of all your senses until the flames in unleashed, engulfed you. And then when it was done it would tear your soul out, robbing you of any breath, of wanting to live. I swore I'd never fall in love again. Not like I had with Willow. That love was all-encompassing. To such an extent, that I lost all sense of where I was and who surrounded me. I let my guard down, and because of that I lost her, and I blamed myself for it. For being stupid enough to live in her perfect bubble. A bubble that was so easily deflated by one of those monsters I swore to protect her from.

Letting love in would only blind me of my true purpose. I'd come here to reap vengeance on the one person who had destroyed that so-called love and made me who I am today. A cold calculating bastard who was self-taught to numb himself from any and all emotions, that included compassion and pain. I dwelled in it and let the love be replaced by vengeance. Allowing it to consume me until it took my breath away, and nothing would get in my way of following through on it. Pain was my pleasure, and I found satisfaction in both receiving and inflicting it. And for the first time, I could tell another person relished in it as much as I did, and that notion was as equally addictive.

I didn't believe that she'd betrayed Petros, those bright blue eyes told another story entirely. One of years of abuse, both mental and physical. A woman who was so adamant in loving a man wouldn't betray him. There was more to the story than she let on and I was going to find out what it was, at any cost.

In the end, it was my decision as to what punishment should be inflicted. She was no longer Petros', and if he ever wanted her back he'd have to go through me first. Clenching my fist, I smiled. If there was ever an occasion to make my mandate known, it was now. I wasn't the one who needed to prove my loyalty. They were.

Every. Single. One of them.

7

JAMESON

I LOOKED at myself in the mirror, straightening out my leather jacket, the President patch was sewn back on and I stared at it for a long moment, trying to decide if I still wanted to be a part of this. I remembered what my father had said to me a few days before his death.

I'm proud of what you've accomplished, son. That title's yours to wear proudly. You earned it.

Bulldog had built this club with his own sweat and blood. He sacrificed everything for this, and he'd chosen me to take over. The question still remained, was I worthy?

I made my way towards the main staircase that ran out to the foyer. I could hear murmurs below, no boisterous laughs or crude jokes. They were mostly quiet, knowing what was coming. I'd had Knuckles call for Church this afternoon, and I was pretty sure that they had all made it in time for roll call.

As soon as I entered the bar, the murmuring stopped. The silence hung heavy over everyone. I wanted for us to meet at the bar because I wanted it to be a place they trusted and felt comfortable in. Not knowing that I was about to make it as uncomfortable as possible.

"I suppose I don't have to shout out over everyone tonight. I'm assuming you all know who I am."

Ayes rang around the room, a few familiar faces nodded up at me. Riddick, the Enforcer I'd met when I first got here, stood at the doorway. Knuckles, stood to my right, Colt in the far back. Tick Tock sat right in front of me, a big grin on his face as he raised the beer bottle to me and took a swig. Bullet, our Secretary nodded at me from the corner. These men had been with us since my father was here, they never left, which made me question their loyalty to me.

Knuckles leaned into me. "You know Forger, the one right next to him, with the greasy mullet and the chains hanging from his belt loop, that's Snake."

I nodded. Snake was Rancid's Sargent At Arms. I wondered if he knew he was going to get axed tonight.

"So let's get some things straight before I continue. I'm sure Colt has somewhat mentioned to you what the deal is here, but let me clarify. I didn't come here to make friends, I lost a lot of my friends along the way. I also don't expect half of you to like me, but I do expect all of you to respect me."

I got a few murmurs for that one. A few of the newer members nodded their heads. "I didn't come here alone. Knuckles here is my right hand and he is now our Sargent At Arms."

"What the fuck?!" Snake stood up, and although I could see Forger whispering for him to sit down, the fool wasn't the type to listen.

"You got somethin' to say?"

"I was given my title by Rancid."

"And that title means shit to me." I looked around the room and hung my head for a second as I thought of the right words. "Let me be clear. Any and all commands that Rancid has imposed on this club are null and void. Starting now."

"We've got codes and rules here." Snake shouted.

I turned to Knuckles. "You believe this?"

"No, SIr."

"Are you saying you're gonna school me on codes and rules? I was fucking raised by them, asshole. Or did you all forget who my father was."

"We'd never forget Bulldog!" Tick tock raised his glass and half the members cheered with him, the others had no clue who the fuck I was talking about, and in truth, that fucking broke my heart.

"For those of you who feel the need to undermine my authority, let me give you a little lesson on the Royal Bastards Code. No one in this room has lived by these codes more than I have. I have lived by them and I have died by them, and no motherfucker is going to say otherwise. Understood?" I glared at Snake and he let out the most sardonic smirk.

"I've heard all about the infamous Elrik Jameson. Murdered his girlfriend in a fit of rage. No self-control, no loyalty. Broke code and was exiled."

I was starting to see red with this motherfucker. "Don't pretend to think you know me. You have no idea who I am or what I am capable of."

"His lackey," he pointed at Knuckles. "Was locked up in the penitentiary state prison and was left to take the blame of his dear President," he purposefully mocked us. "And then he was left to rot in a jail cell."

"Watch your fucking tongue," Knuckles' hoarse command meant he was about to snap.

"You come in here all high and mighty thinkin' you're better than all of us, but you're nothing. Your daddy gave you a fucking title and you let it go to waste."

Knuckles started to move, but I placed my hand on his chest, stopping him. A dark calm swept over me and I could sense that this motherfucker wanted a fight. I believe he was about to become an example.

"You done spitting out your vile shit?"

"Rancid will get out and when he does..."

"I'd be very careful with the next words that come out of your snout." Knuckles moved to my side as I stood up.

"When he does, I can't wait to see how he's going to cut your fucking head off."

"Well now, you sure are a dumb fuck."

Snake just snarled in response and I signaled to Styx in the back followed by Knuckles who immediately moved into action. They dragged him into a chair, he was a big guy and he struggled but Riddick chimed in to help, holding him down. Styx held him in a chokehold as I approached.

"I think you all deserve to know what happens to traitors around here." I leaned in to look Snake in the eye. "I don't believe I introduced myself as I should have."

"You're gonna die."

"What, didn't they tell you?" I aimed the gun at his knee. "I already died a long time ago. Just came back from the dead to pay y'all a visit. Guess it was your turn to go first." I popped a bullet into his kneecap and watched him fall over, wailing in agony. I crouched over him, tipping his chin up with my gun. "Now did I not tell you not to underestimate me."

"Fuck you!" He spat out, and aiming the gun, I took a step back and popped a bullet into his second kneecap." His wails turned to whimpers of pain and I signaled to Riddick to take him away.

"Don't take him too far, we're not done with him yet." I turned to the rest of the members and swept my gun from left to right. "Anybody else want a turn?"

I focused on where Forger had been standing, but the son of a bitch disappeared. Goddammit, I wanted to make the biggest example out of him tonight, but that would, unfortunately, have to wait.

"Like I was saying, I didn't come here for you to like me. I came here to do my father's bidding. The Royal Bastards was my home and I expect it to run as such. That means respect runs both ways. As you can see, I really don't like traitors or liars, so I would suggest y'all watch your tongue around me."

A collective, Yes, Sir, resounded around the room. "I ain't here to ride this like a dictatorship, but there will be some changes made. Like I was sayin' before I was so rudely interrupted. Knuckles will now be the Sargent At Arms, Riddick and Styx will follow right under him. Tick Tock you still the Road Captain?"

"That's right."

"I thought you would have left."

"No, Prez. This has always been my home. Couldn't leave and let it go to shit, ya know what I mean."

I nodded. "Good to hear that."

I turned to Bullet. "Is that the same for you too."

"Yes, Sir."

I paced the room and he knew what he had to do without me even sayin' it. "I'm stepping down as VP. Jameson has taken his Presidency back and he's in the right to do what he wants to do."

"You sound mighty chivalrous, Colt. I suggest you stop playing the hero and get down on your fucking knees."

He stared at me, and he damn well knew it wasn't going to be as easy as it thought it would be. Slowly, he approached me, and keeping his eyes focused on me, he dropped to his knees.

"VP was always too shiny a title for you. I'mma go ahead and drop you down to Prospect, see if you could learn to crawl back up the ladder again. But before I do that…"

I brought over the wooden billie club and held it in front of Colt's face. "You know what the punishment is, don't you?"

His eyes met mine, but he didn't say a word. A curt nod was the only response I received from him. He knew damn well I was being lenient with him, and that he deserved more than a simple beating for what he had done to me. But this would suffice for now.

Holding up the club, I swung, hitting him square on the jaw. Each member stood up and took a whack at him. I could see their transgressions as they swung, but they were also showing their loyalty to me. Colt shouted out as he raised a hand to defend himself and the billie club landed on his finger, snapping it back. Again and again, he was hit on his ribs and back, and I knew he'd get a few black and blues and a couple of broken ribs. When everyone took their turn I ordered for someone to take him to the hospital. I wanted to teach him a lesson, not have him die on me.

As he was being dragged out he managed to whisper something to me. "I hope you're satisfied."

I stared at all of them and I had to admit, satisfaction came at a price. But it was so damn worth it.

Knuckles once again approached me. He never questioned me, just followed orders. But he'd told me he didn't want to participate in Colt's punishment and I respected that. Colt was always good to him and took care of him as needed when he was down and behind bars. He didn't mention him as he came up to me, a solemn look in his eye.

"What is it?"

"What do you want us to do with Snake?"

"Where is he?"

"Out back on the grass, we didn't want his blood seeping into the floorboards."

"Get as much information out of him as you can. I don't give a shit what you do with him after. But I am curious to know what kind of trafficking ring Rancid was running and how the fuck he was getting these girls out to Seattle. I want to know how close those fucking Russians are to knockin' on our door."

"I'm on it, Prez."

"And Knuckles," he turned to me. "Make sure that mother-fucker disappears when you're done with him."

He nodded, a twisted gleam in his eye. He was about to dish out some serious punishment and I wish I could partake, but I needed to get my hands dirty with the new toy I had out back. She required a visit tonight.

8

SADIE

"Please."

I shivered as he ripped my clothes off slowly. The blade cutting smoothly through the fabric. What he couldn't cut off, he ripped off. I swung on the chains, back and forth, my body exposed and drenched in freezing cold water. It's what he'd used to wake me up. He'd looked enraged as I spattered water all over his face, and I knew I would be his target today. The one he'd take all his anger out on.

He'd dragged me out of bed and as much as I struggled to get out of his grasp, his hold on me was too strong. Pulling my wrists up, he pinned me to the cell bars as he chained me up. The pulley was hooked to the bars that ran along the top of the cell, and slowly he pulled on the chain, raising me up until my feet couldn't touch the ground. My arms strained above me, the chains cutting into my wrists. The pain told me I was still alive, and I focused on it.

His eyes roamed over me, the blade cold as it traced my flesh, raising goosebumps and causing me to tremble. He ran the blade down my body and I gasped as he slid it between my legs. I bit my lip and whimpered in fear as he flicked his wrist, the dull edge of the knife slid through me easily. Flicking across my clit and making me flinch.

He dragged the knife out and brought it to his tongue, growling as he slid it across his pink muscle. Tasting me.

"You're twisted."

"Is there any other way to be?"

"Why don't you just let me go? You know it's ridiculous to have me here. I've done nothing wrong."

"You're right. But see, Sadie, I figured something out last night." I stared at him as he dragged the tip of the blade along the underside of my arms. "I like you."

"What?" I breathed.

He walked up in front of me, breasts only inches from his mouth, and I suddenly felt a yearning in my loins.

"I needed a new toy to play with. And tag, you're it."

"Let me go!" I shook on the chains and he grinned at me.

"You're going to talk to me, Sadie."

"I don't know what you want me to tell you."

"You're keeping something from me. It's simple. Your only way out is to tell me the truth." His hot breath coated my nipples and I shivered as he grinned up at me, taking a quick lick and making me bite my lip.

What was it about this man? He was so unnerving and wrong in every sense of the word, yet he fascinated me in the most perverse of ways.

"I am not keeping anything from you."

He pressed the blade to my neck and I swallowed nervously. His hand ran down my tummy and across my hip before sliding between my legs.

"No," I gave out a moan coated in shame.

Whatever the hell this man was doing to me, my traitorous body was enjoying.

"I don't take lightly to liars."

"I don't know what you want me to tell you."

"Everything," he whispered against my lips as his calloused fingers slid into my wetness. My mouth parted and he bit down on my bottom lip, my arms strained on the chains as he dipped the tips of his fingers in and out of my needy hole.

When we both looked down, a tattoo of a woman stared back at me. His forearm flexed and she moved as his fingers began to stroke me. I gasped as his thumb swiped across my sensitive bud and I shook, the chains rattling above me.

"Such a slick little pussy. Am I exciting you, Sadie? Does the thought of me touching you so intimately get you off?"

I whimpered as my body reacted to his deep husky tone. "Leave me alone."

He flicked my clit once again and the sound of the chains announced just how much my body loved his touch. Just how perfectly it jerked alive.

"I h-hate you," I moaned as my body slowly gave into him.

I honestly did hate him. I hated that I was at his mercy. I hated that he had me locked up in this cell. And above all, I hated the fact that he knew exactly how to touch my body in order to make it bend to his will. I also hated the fact that as much as I fought him, I wanted more.

"Fuck, you move so sensually. Just look at how your cunny welcomes me?"

I whimpered, his filthy words igniting me. I shouldn't feel this way about this man.

This stranger.

I didn't even know his name, yet I felt like I knew him completely. I felt what he felt, the pain, the heartache, the need to feel something more.

"I think about you on my cock, Sadie. I think about this wet pussy sliding down my dick as I watch you get off on it."

"Oh!" I yelled out as his thumb circled my clit.

Why did that confession affect me so much?

I should feel repulsed, but instead, here I am, needing more.

"But I'm supposed to hurt you, Sadie." The tip of the blade slid down my torso and I gasped as he nicked me, so expertly. A sole crimson drop seeped out from beneath the shallow nick, and traveled slowly down my body, across my belly until it dripped onto his hand. Those strong hands that knew exactly how to light me on fire.

He looked down, licking his lips as he mixed my blood with my cum. "Fuck, you look so sexy right now. So fucking pure."

"You're fucking crazy," I hitched a breath as his eyes met mine, two turbulent hues arousing me in so many ways.

What was he doing to me?

What kind of sick twisted mind game was this?

Keep your resilience, Sadie. It's all you have left.

Grabbing my neck, he squeezed tightly, cutting off my air. The blade clattered loudly as it hit the concrete. I gasped as his fingers slid into me. Thick, long, fingers that curled into me so exquisitely. My body shook, and with it, the chains announced my convulsions.

I moaned, my head falling back as he fucked me, his fingers driving into me in a ceaseless rhythm. My body relinquished itself to the pleasure he was giving me, my screams only meant for him.

I hung my head forward and he pressed his forehead to my own while his forearm moved back and forth, his thumb rolling against my tight clit. I hung there, helpless, enjoying every second of his hands on me.

"I want you to cum for me, Sadie. I want to watch you lose that control you covet so dearly," he whispered against my neck before taking a pebbled nipple into his mouth and swirling his tongue over it, biting down on it to cause me just the right amount of pain. His other hand ran along my body, as if though he were memorizing every curve and crevice.

"You're so fucking beautiful," he breathed and ran kisses across my breasts and taking his time down my body.

I gasped at the odd sensations that ran through me. My head told me I needed to run, to hide from this man. But my body lit up at his touch and begged me to stay.

I cried out as he got to his knees before me. He perched my legs on his shoulders alleviating the pressure off my wrists, only to immediately be tortured by his mouth. The way his tongue swept across each of my pussy lips, delicately parting them to take a long lick along my center, brought a thrill up my spine. My thighs trembled as he gripped my ass, pressing me into his mouth. I cried out again, wishing I knew his name.

His hunger was evident in the way he sucked on me, the way he groaned as his tongue wriggled inside of me. Dragging my juices out and lapping them up, like a dog would drink water. Curled tongue, heavy pants, and the most incessant slurping I'd ever heard. He hissed along with me as he inserted those same two fingers he'd been torturing me with. I could only hear the sound of his zipper being pulled down. And then his growl against my pussy lips as he brought pleasure to himself while he had me perched on his tongue.

The thought of him jerking his cock off, had me rotating my lips on his shoulders. Rubbing my pussy along his chin and tongue. I cried out as he flicked my clit, circling it expertly until I was a submissive mess.

"Fuuuuck," he ran his hands up my body, cupping my breasts and squeezing the tips of my nipples as I began to reach that sought out climax. He took one last lick of me, and I whimpered wantonly as he stood before me. My eyes finally getting a look at his cock. He was thick and swollen, his mushroom head was red and seeping white cream. My pussy pulsed as it watched him pull on it. He'd squeeze tightly and I imagined him coming closer and sliding into me. His dark green eyes took their fill of me, there was no brightness to them, just lascivious desire. And I arched and reveled in it. No man had ever looked at me that way, especially not Petros.

No.

This man wanted me. He did not hide it. Not one bit. And there was something so sexy in that.

He came up to me then and I shivered as he dragged his nails lightly across my lower abdomen, sneaking his hand right between my legs. I gasped as his fingers played along my clit. My body shook.

He leaned forward, his breath on my neck. "I want you to cum on my cock."

I looked down and watched as his cock slid between my legs. I shivered as he dragged it through my slit, stroking my pussy with each thrust of his hips. He never entered me, just played with me until I was a sobbing, screaming mess, my body tightened from the feel of his hard dick sliding through my pussy, parting my swollen lips, and jabbing again and again over my sensitive clit. I unashamedly came all over his cock, just like he wanted me to. His dirty words elicited a perverse response from me, and I simply hung there, my head flung forward and limp as he grunted and jacked off, spewing his hot load all over my body.

He stood there for a minute, admiring his artwork before he reached back and slowly brought me down to the ground. I was too worn out to stand, and he came up to me and unchained me, carrying me into his arms and placing me onto the thin mattress. I was surprised when he slid in behind me. I don't why I did it, but I turned into him, pressing my nose against his neck as he wrapped his arms around me.

"Will you ever let me go?" I'm not sure why I asked, but there was something inside of me that needed to know.

"I don't think I'll ever be able to let you go, Sadie." He pressed his lips to my forehead and squeezed me tighter. "I don't think I'll be able to do that."

Tears fell down my cheeks and onto the front of his shirt. I cried silently as I was held by this man. He'd done the most unimaginable things to me in these last couple weeks. He'd wanted to break me, and somehow he did just that because in his arms I finally felt protected and wanted. I felt like he truly couldn't let me go, but not because of fearing Petros, but for another reason entirely, and he was struggling with it as much as I was. I thought I was in love with Petros, but in these last few days, I realized that it was just lust. Because I was fighting to be loved, and you don't fight for that. You either are loved or you aren't.

My life wasn't easy. I'd been abused by my father, beaten by my mother when she found out. Her jealousy was overbearing and I had inherited that emotion because I was forcing myself on men who weren't right for me. I thought if I could just get my way, I'd be happy, but that's not how love works. And this man...this man whom I'd just met, had shown me more love in one phrase than anyone else had in my entire life.

As much as I wanted to believe that my mind wasn't as fucked up as it seemed, it had become nearly impossible. Whatever this man was doing to me was affecting me in more ways than I wanted it to, and he was bringing out demons I'd never spoken of to anyone. I kept them buried deep down inside, hidden from sight because if I let them out they'd destroy any good in my life. But this man wanted them, he begged me for them with each heated touch and wet sweep of his tongue. He called them out and they were more than willing to play with his own.

Wrapping my arms around him, I finally let myself get lost in his embrace. And for the first time in my life, I felt truly accepted and not just for my body, but for these twisted feelings, I harbored inside.

I no longer felt ashamed.
On the contrary.
I felt like I belonged.

✣ 9 ✣

JAMESON

THIS WOMAN WAS ENCOMPASSING every fucking second of my life. Precious seconds where I needed to be planning my revenge not on thinking about her fresh pussy so wet and needy for me.

I walked down the streets of New Orleans, the moon shining down on my shadow. I was doing a favor for Voodoo who was down in Ankeny, Iowa. He was one of the Enforcers for the Chapter, but his granddaddy had been a co-founder of the Royal Bastards, and he'd run with my Father. As I said, the RBMC was family, and that meant that blood coursed through us too.

Voodoo had recently reached out to me asking me to keep an eye out on his grandmother. Some shit was going down and he needed to protect her. Adelaide Laveaux was one of the sweetest old ladies I'd ever met, and one of the most dangerous. While her grandson was a deep believer in Hoodoo, Ms. Adelaide worked her magic in Voodoo. I used to be afraid of her when I was a kid, telling stories about the witch who lived in the swamps, and I had no clue how true those stories were until I met her. She was beyond enchanting, she was Bayou's Voodoo Priestess.

I decided to go down and visit her tonight. It had been years since I'd seen her and I was in need of some guidance. I was sure she would be able to read me like a book. I had made a deep connection with Voodoo during my exile. He'd reached out to me and had expressed how he didn't agree with what had gone down. He told me that if I ever needed anything, that he could bind the evil spirits and clear my path to see my purpose. He always had a way of bringing his beliefs into the conversation.

After so many conversations and teachings on the subject, a box arrived one day at my doorstep. In it was a Tarot card deck and a note from Voodoo.

Always respect them and they will show you the way.

After a while, I became curious about the religion, and with no one to keep me company but myself, I started to look at Voodoo in another light and to see the Tarot as more than just cards. It became an obsession to learn everything about them. What they signified. They're history, their readings. But it wasn't just about learning the cards, it was digging into something deeper. Something that pulled at me.Something so dark I had to protect myself from it at every turn.

Adelaide had once given me a warning and I didn't heed it until years later.

It was dawn and I was seated at a local restaurant, eating crepes and contemplating my first kill. I kept staring out the window at the people rushing by, wondering why it didn't bother me to take a life as much as it had bothered Ian. To me, it had been natural to pull the trigger in order to survive. What troubled me wasn't the kill, it was the fact that I didn't even flinch as I took that life.

I remember she came up to me out of nowhere and whispered the message in my ear. "The Devil's got his eye on your soul, boy. Take care where your path leads you. Veer away from evil and follow the light. She'll lead you out of the darkness."

That had always stayed with me, even to this day. I had even gotten protection spells carved into my body. The tattoo on my left was inked by a witch. The pyramid signified protection, and instilled with it were the four levels.

To know. To dare. To will. To keep silent.

The tattoo on my right arm was that of my Willow, her face carved into the Tarot card of Death. She was my ultimate protector. Along my back, I wore the symbol of Papa Legba. Carefully designed to fit across my shoulders. I figured why should I fear the devil, when I could have him by my side, opening gates and allowing me to walk through.

But tonight, everything was clouding my judgments, and I needed clarity. Stepping onto the boat, I quietly made my way out into the swamps. Our dear Adelaide lived hidden among the Bayou trees in a quiet cabin off the east side of the river. No one knew she existed out here, only the few who made sure she was safe and well protected.

Thirty minutes later I spotted the light of the cabin. I forgot how dark it could get out here in the swamps. The sound of frogs and the bubbles coming up from the water alerted me that I wasn't alone. There was always a beast lurking around at this time of night.

I secured the boat and made my way up the muddy road and up to her door. I knocked twice, just as Voodoo had told me to do. The door opened and the Voodoo Priestess, already expecting me, welcomed me with open arms.

"*Beau diable!*" She reached out and swept her arms around me, hugging me tightly. "You finally come around to see me. Let me take a look at ya'."

She pulled me away, her eyes narrowing as she assessed me. The wrinkles were profound along her skin, telling a long story with intricate details of sorrow, loss, and love. Her eyes were an opaque blue, cataracts had caused them to film over in a gray hue. She pursed her lips as she ran her hands up and down my arms, as if she were feeling my aura. Then she gripped my hand, slammed the door, and led me towards the back of the house and through a doorway. At the far end there stood a room, and moving over a curtain of red and black beads, I entered her sanctuary.

"Sit. You have had a long journey."

"Now, it was only thirty minutes, Ms. Adelaide."

She reached out and tilted my chin up. "Do not play games here, Elrik." She swiped her hand gently down my face. "Your facade doesn't work here."

I sighed as she moved to her temple, lighting up more candles and bringing over her tarot deck. She wielded a delicate silver knife in her right hand. Having silver in hand restored stability in a person's spiritual energy. It also protected her from any dark energy that surrounded me, reflecting the energy back to where it came from.

She cut the deck and without another word, she waved her hand and had me touch the cards. Slowly she began to reveal the cards one by one. When she was done, she concentrated on them, the knife consistently being whirled around her fingers. So easily she maneuvered it and I wondered if it had ever spilled any blood.

"Ahhh, there is a woman. Ahhh, *belle femme*. She will give you very much love. Too much love." She pointed to the card above. "Ezilie protects you."

"Should I pursue that?"

She nodded. "She is good for you."

She pressed a finger to her lips and frowned as the card of Death followed by the Devil appeared. "Ohhh," she breathed deeply. "You have darkness around you. Papa Legba calls out to you."

Pulling out another card she shakes her head. Written

along the bottom of the card is the word Ruin, and I instinctively know it's the card of deep betrayal and bitterness.

Looking up at me she leans in and whispers, as if telling me a secret. "This darkness is not good. With it comes a change in tides."

She pulled out another card and nodded. The card is that of Dance. I stared at the cards, quietly assessing them myself. She saw things I didn't, that much I knew. I didn't have the power she wielded just yet. But I felt it emanating from her. I was sensitive to it and she knew it too.

"You will dance. You will triumph but at a cost." She points to the woman above. "Betrayal is at the heart of the cards, and a bad comes for you, beau diable. He wants to destroy all the good you have."

She reached out and grabbed my hands. "Do not turn your back, for it will get stabbed."

Lifting the Empress card she emphasized on it. "Protect her. At all costs. She is that line between love and death. Choose love, Elrik. Love always wins."

I stared at her for a moment as she prayed over the cards, she did her ritual and as I watched and heard her prayers, a sense of peace came over me. I inhaled deeply the roots she was burning and felt lightheaded.

"Come," she took my hand again and led me out to the living room. A heaviness lifted off my shoulders and I took a deep breath as if waking from a dream.

"I have cleansed you. Now go. See clearly now."

"So easily you dismiss me."

"This all you needed from me. If I need you I will let you know. Now go. Leave me to pray."

"Adelaide," I looked down at her, and I could feel the concern etched in my brow.

She patted my hand and smiled. "It's not my time yet, sweet Elrik. Voodoo exaggerates."

I was hesitant about leaving her, but I also knew she was well aware of the dangers she was in. She'd already learned her future and she'd accepted that fate while Voodoo wanted to change it. But one didn't change fate's path, you simply followed it as it changed you. It made me wonder if fate's path had led me to that cell and to the woman who now filtered through in my future.

10

SADIE

I NEEDED to get out of here. Enough was enough. I still didn't know who this man was, but he was slowly taking over my life. Every day I wondered if he'd come to see me, and when he didn't, I suddenly found myself missing him. I was worn out and exhausted, and all I wanted was to go home.

Home.

What a ridiculous notion.

I didn't have a home. Everything was taken from me when Petros sent me away. My love, my home, my friends, everything. I had nowhere to go. Nowhere to be but right here, stuck in this cell. I stared at the food that Styx had brought me earlier. It stood at the foot of the bed, and I was grateful that at least I had a roof over my head and food in my belly.

There were so many nights throughout my childhood where I didn't even have a crumb of anything to eat. I was living in my car when Petros found me and brought me into the club-house. He was my knight in shining armor, how could I not have fallen in love with him. But I was just a plaything to him. A bitch that warmed up his bed. He was very clear with me on that. But I still hoped, like the silly girl that I am. I still hoped he'd want me. That he'd one day realized he loved me and would come and claim me as his Old Lady.

He always thought I was after that. The title. If he only knew, that's not all I wanted. I needed him. But that was my mistake to bear. My heart was to be destroyed. I reached out and brought the sandwich to my lips, I moaned as the flavor of chicken salad reached my tongue.

"You moan like that even when I'm not around?"

My heart leaped into my throat as he entered into the light. I watched him, quietly setting my food down. I wondered what it was he wanted tonight. There had to be another way to get through to him. To make him understand that I didn't belong here. He stepped up to the bars and I met him on the other side, angry with him for keeping me locked up in here.

"Jameson," I whispered his name for the first time. Styx mentioned him as he came through the doors and I was so grateful to finally know who I was dealing with. This was the infamous Elrik Jameson, President of the New Orleans National Chapter. The man whom everyone talked so much about. His presence alone made me shudder, I could only imagine what his enemies felt.

His eyes met mine as I said his name and he gave me a slow smile, seeming to like his name on my lips. "I see they told you who I am. Did they also tell you why I'm here?"

"They didn't have to, I could see it in your eyes. Vengeance speaks for itself."

He narrowed his gaze on me. "You have no idea what that means."

"Petros told me what they did to you. The only reasoning I could see for your return is just that. It's what I would do."

I placed my hand around the steel bar, keeping myself from reaching out and touching him, and he suddenly wrapped his hand around mine, simply watching as our fingers interlocked. It was only a brief moment, but in it, I saw his pain. I wondered if he'd ever spoken about it to anyone, or maybe I was the only one in his world who truly understood it.

Somehow, in all this mess, I had a sense that I needed to protect this man. To be by his side. As much as he wanted to show me otherwise, I knew he wasn't all bad. I remembered that Petros didn't get along with him, but in the end, he still thought what had been done was wrong. He'd told me that he was a naive kid who wasn't ready to become President, but his father believed otherwise. I wondered what he was like as a child. Was he happy? Was he loved?

"Please, let me out, Elrik."

"You know I can't do that."

"Why not?" A tear escaped down my cheek and he reached out to catch it.

"Because if I do, then I'll be considered disloyal, and I can't have that right now."

"So you're gonna keep me here forever?"

He shrugged. "For as long as I have to, yes."

"I have to suffer because you like to fuck me. You're just like them all, wanting to own me. I don't belong to anyone, Jameson. Least of all you."

His jaw clenched and his grip tightened around my hand. "You were brought to me to prove a point."

"Punishing the weak? Is that what the Royal Bastards are about? Is that the type of points that make you get your kicks off."

He gripped the steel bars and reached out with one hand, gripping my hair and pulling my head forward. He pressed his forehead to mine and held me for a long minute before he spoke.

"Tell me what it is you're keeping from me."

"Why do you think I'm keeping something from you?"

"Because Hart swears he didn't fuck you."

I turned my head away and he reached through the bars

and pulled my chin forward, forcing me to look at him. "Did you fuck him?"

"Would you care if I did?" I was angry now. Angry that Hart was out free and alive, and I was stuck in here.

"What kind of question is that?"

Something came over me, and I reached out and ran my hand across his crotch, squeezing his semi-hard cock. "Doesn't seem like it."

He growled, wrapping one hand around my neck, the other behind my head and yanking me forward just enough so that he had access to my mouth, his hot breath hitting my lips.

"Don't test me, Woman."

"I can sweeten the deal for you, Elrik. Let me be your whore. That's what you want isn't it?" I gripped his cock harder, stroking him. "You just want a toy to fuck."

He growled as he spun me around, trapping me back against the bars.

"You want to play with the devil? Because he doesn't fucking need to ask, he just takes whatever the fuck he wants."

His hand slid up to squeeze my breasts and my body betrayed me once again. I kept fighting it, but there was no doubt I belonged to this man. I gasped as he squeezed the tips of my nipples into two hardened peaks, and I gripped the bars tightly, my tits jutting out and pressing against his hands. Uttering a curse, his hands wrapped around my neck, my head now trapped against the steel bars.

"Take your pants off," he gritted, slightly squeezing the sides of my throat.

My hands were shaking as I fumbled with my zipper. If this is what he wanted then I'd go through with it. It was the only way to gain his trust.

Wasn't it?

"Now!"

I slowly dropped my jeans and holding on to the bars for

balance, I slowly stepped out of them. Unable to move any further, I kicked them aside. Hastily, he grabbed my arms and twisted them back between the bars. I yelped from the sharp pain that ran across my shoulder blades, but he didn't show any sign of stopping. All I could hear was his sharp breaths. He wasn't going to make this pleasant for me. I was here for a reason, and he reminded me of this as he handcuffed my wrists, keeping me secure against the bars. I had a feeling this would be a lesson I'd never forget.

His hands ran down my body as if he were assessing his property. Yanking my shirt up, my breasts fell out and he grunted, pulling on the fabric until it was up beneath my armpits. He tugged on it, pulling it through the bars and using it to keep me still. His hands came around me and I found myself trapped with nowhere to go. My hands restrained and my body arched back as his hands took their fill of my flesh. I shivered at the thought that I was about to become his once again.

This is what you asked for, Sadie.

Now accept the consequences.

Grabbing my hips, he slammed my ass back against the bars. His hands immediately diving between my legs, fingers running their path across my wet panty line. His rumble was animalistic and raw. Pure sex came from it, and I delivered a moan.

The flick of his switchblade kept me on alert, and my thighs shook as he traced the tip of it against my core.

"Such a good girl," he breathed out steadily as he gently slid the blade beneath my panty line.

I never thought I'd be into this sort of thing. Petros was rough and passionate, but Jameson was deliberate and methodical. He took pleasure in my fear, and if he could make me cum as I screamed in fright, that would be his ultimate satisfaction.

He slapped my thigh and I inhaled a sharp breath. "Don't. Move. Unless you want to bleed."

He gently stroked the flesh he'd smacked and pressed his nose against me. "God, how I love when you bleed."

I whimpered as he flicked his wrist and the blade tore away at my panties, letting me know that it was sharp and unyielding. He continued to drag the blade across my slit, flicking the dull edge across my clit and I screamed, yet trembled from excitement. His words were meant to fuck with your mind. To incite fear and make you believe he wanted to hurt you. It had become my ultimate turn on.

He hissed and grabbed a handful of my ass cheek, biting down on it as he continued to drag the edge of the knife ever so slowly against my inner thighs. I pressed my head back against the bars and took deep uneven breaths as he ran his tongue along my soft flesh. The path between pleasure and pain was slowly blurring.

"So fucking pretty," he stuck his tongue between the crevice of my ass and took a long wet lick of me, right before he flicked my clit with the blade again. I screamed and began to sob, confused as to how afraid I was, and yet how wet I'd become.

He chuckled against my slit, his breath fluttered over me, sending hot delicious tingles all through my body. God, this man could do things to me. How was this possible?

"So fucking perfect," he growled before placing his hand on my back. His demand was gentle as he silently ordered me to bend over slightly. The slap of the blade on my inner thighs signaled for me to spread my legs.

And I did.

Oh, how I did.

And when his fingers played along my lips, a barely-there touch that had me shivering, I whispered his name in pure need. That blade dragged along my pussy, outlining each pouty lip and flicking against my clit. I screamed again, going on tiptoes, and that's when he grabbed me, slamming my ass back against the bars, his arms wrapping around my thighs, holding me secure as he feasted on me. Harsh persistent lashes of his tongue on my clit that had me yelling out his name in between ragged pants of adrenaline which coursed through my veins. I arched back, offering my ass to him and he moaned as he stroked, and sucked. His lips pursing over my clit and my body jolted as he bit down. My scream echoed through the room, yet we both were filled with the undeniable truth that no one would be able to hear me.

No one.

Suddenly I felt something smooth and metallic slide against my opening and I hung my head as I knew what he would do next. Instead of fighting it, my body welcomed it. My breath caught in my throat as the handle of the switchblade was pushed into me, over and over, fucking me on it as he continued to force his perverse needs on me.

I couldn't help but spread my legs and stretch out for him, the sensation was incredible and I couldn't hide the pussy juice that dripped down the handle. His tongue ran up along the crevice of my ass and flicked around my puckered hole, before he went right back to my pussy, hungrily lapping and sucking on it. My legs began to shake, my breath leaving me, and I let out a strangled moan as I came for him, struggling against the restraints that held me confined to that cell. I rose into that assault of emotions until I couldn't take it anymore.

But he still wasn't done with me yet.

His hand wrapped around my neck as his presence radiated heat at my back. I heard the sound of his zipper and hitched a sharp breath as suddenly, his bare cock slid along my wet slit. It felt so thick and hard as the tip parted my lips.

"You want to play the whore with me, Sadie?"

I cried out as he grabbed my tits and squeezed. "You may have been a whore back in Lincoln, but here you're mine," he

INKED IN VENGEANCE

whispered as his cock strained inside of me, stretching me out on it. "And I don't treat my women like whores. No. I worship them. And I give them exactly what they want."

I shivered as he sunk his cock into me, taking me completely.

"Your pussy knows who it's made for. You feel how tight it grips me. You wanted me that badly, Woman?" He bit down on my shoulder. "Such a needy cunny, dripping and ready for her man."

Gripping my neck, he held me tight against the cell bars as he began to slide in and out of my eager pussy. I whimpered as he took me. There was no denying the fact that this man consumed me. My body loved every second of his torture.

"I want you to know, Sadie, that if you ever decide to go behind my back and ride a cock other than mine, I will make you suffer a very painful death."

I moaned as he pulled out of me and slammed back into me hard, fucking me through the steel bars. His grip on my throat tightened as he rammed into me over and over again. I didn't want to enjoy it. My intention was not to play into his perverse games. But as his cock slid in, settling deep inside me, and his hand came around to my clit, stroking my pleasure, I knew there was no other way in or out. This man owned my body completely.

I shouted out as I gave him my release. My body jerked forward, my ass straining against the bars as he held my hips and fucked me into submission. The sounds of sex permeated the shed, reverberating against the metal walls, and I gave myself to him, sliding myself back onto his cock as I was held captured by him.

I listened to his ragged breaths, the hiss of air through his teeth as I squeezed him. The way he touched me, with a gentle force that was meant to instill ownership, yet it asserted the fact that I was safe. He was struggling with himself, I knew this because of the way he fucked me. He was holding back. His dick slid into me, stretching me so fully before pulling out and teasing me. I wasn't just a fuck toy for him, he wanted to take my pleasure, as much as he could. I wasn't just a cumslut for him. No. This was him staking his claim on me and making sure I knew who I belonged to.

He tugged on the shirt, holding me up as he slowed down his pace. "I want your honesty, Sadie. What are you keeping from me?"

"I can't tell you," I moaned as he slid in deep, grinding up into me.

"Yes you can, Beautiful. You can trust me."

I gasped as he slid out and rammed back into me and at that moment I was afraid. Afraid he'd let me go. Afraid I'd never see him again.

"No," I breathed and he roared in anger. His thrusts were brutal, his hands squeezed my hips, they would leave bruises from his assault.

His hand came up to my neck, and he squeezed as he fucked me. I was helpless once again, and as much as I didn't want to, the wave of pleasure that crashed through us both was so intense, I blacked out.

When I came to, I was lying on the cot clothed in only a fresh shirt. As I moved my thighs I moaned feeling the slickness of his cum mixed with mine. Sitting up, I pressed a hand to my head feeling light-headed. I could barely remember what happened. He must have squeezed just enough that I passed out. The thought disturbed me. I slowly made my way across the cell, to the basin of water they had for me, and I quickly cleaned up. As I passed the cloth between my legs I moaned at the sensitivity there.

I could have just told him the truth, but if I did then what would happen. Petros wanted me punished, probably dead. If I told the truth, he might take my life, or even worse, tell me to go. I wasn't ready to go. I wanted so desperately to belong some-where, to somebody. In this short amount of time, Jameson had taught me what it meant to truly be craved by a man. And that craving was addictive because it fucked me up so severely, I wanted to stay by this crazy man's side.

I slumped down on the mattress and stared down at the concrete floor. I couldn't do this forever. I had to tell him the truth. It was the only way for him to know that I trusted him. What he would do with that trust is what I was afraid of.

Would he truly break me or would he keep me like he said he would?

I wasn't sure.

And the uncertainty was killing me.

11

RANCID

I WALKED out the doors of the state prison, shielding my eyes from the bright sunlight. I breathed in the clean air, taking in a hint of freshly cut grass. Fuck it felt good to be free.

Forger met me out front, the keys to my truck in his hand.

Walking up to him, I put my hand on his shoulder. "Good to know I still have people I can count on."

"Not as many as you'd think, Prez."

I smirked. "So he's taken over?"

"Yes, Sir."

"Who brought him back?"

"Colt did, Sir."

"Fucking, traitor. But we'll make sure he gets his, won't we?"

Forger's eyes grew wide and then he nodded vigorously. "Yes, Prez. Absolutely."

Such a good henchman. Stupid fuck had no clue he'd also be a part of the deceased as soon as this whole thing was done. He was just as dispensable as the rest of them.

"Jameson called Church a few nights ago. He took his patch and his title. Told him he was going back to Prospect and needed to earn his rightful place again. He had the others beat him."

"Well now, the boy came bearing some balls, I see."

"Word's spreading quickly. Seems he's already sent word out to a few of the other Chapters. I'm not gonna lie, Prez. Most seem happy to have him back. Just a few of us were against him, but after what he did to Snake, I don't think anyone will go against his demands."

"What did he do to Snake?"

"Let's just say the gators had a feast that night. I told him to keep his mouth shut, but he didn't listen. He paid the price for being stupid."

"Is that so?" I stared at Forger who continued to blabber as we drove out of sight.

"You shouldn't underestimate Jameson, he's got some dark shit going on in his head. Some real fucked up shit."

I nodded as he told me everything that was going on in the Chapter. Forger had always been on my side, supposedly looking out for my well-being. More than I could say for half the fuckers out there. But I knew he was only looking out for his own hyde. In the end, it was in his best interest to stay by my side, especially since he'd been falsifying records and signatures in order for us to get Jameson's cut of the money that was inherited from Bulldog. There were only a few more steps to take, and the clubhouse would also be in my name.

"So the motherfucker thinks he can just sweep right in and take what's mine."

"He keeps to himself for the most part. And besides, I'd say he's become obsessed with the little pet that was left at our doorstep. A traitorous bitch sent by Petros."

That caught my attention, especially since I did love to have pets. Of course, having them was the main reason why I got stuck in this shit in the first place. Gamble was my favorite pet of them all, young virgin, tight, and fucking rebellious. Fuck how I loved when they fought me. Giving me a reason to gag and rope them up. In the end, the more they begged the harder I got until they were filled up with my seed. Too bad I had to get rid of them when I was done. The Russians wanted virgin pussies and I couldn't send them out. So I destroyed them and dumped their pieces in the Bayou hoping the Gators would devour them. It was a stupid move on my part. Next time I knew what to do. You simply burn the corpses.

"Now that's interesting. Tell me more about this pet."

"They keep her out in the metal barn. Styx is in charge of taking care of her, bringing her food and shit. I've been watching them. Seems Jameson likes to get his dick wet time and time again. Fuck, who wouldn't, she's somethin' else."

I vaguely remember Petros, holding onto a girl at his club-house. She was off-limits to everyone and he kept her well hidden. I always wanted a taste but never did get around to have a piece of her. Seems like my future now holds a goldilocks with a sweet pussy.

We drove down the old Louisiana back roads, heading to a safe house I had set aside for times like these. It was set right in between the swamps, down a twisted road that people hated traveling on. It was an old rackety thing, barely a cot and a microwave, enough to stay a few nights.

Forger seemed fidgety as he set some bags on the kitchen counter. "Speak your mind."

"Prez, I'm sorry to ask this, but how long do you have?"

"Just enough to cut that motherfucker in half and get the fuck out of NOLA."

"I'm sorry to say this Prez, but I think it would be best if you just let us handle it. The FBI will come looking for you as soon as they find out."

Forger wasn't wrong, but I wasn't leaving until I made sure Elrik Jameson was six feet under. I should have put him in the ground years ago, but I was advised against it. Instead, I made an example out of him, but of course, he didn't learn his lesson.

When I got sentenced, I immediately called my contacts in Russia. All they had to do was send me the money, and I paid off the Warden. Overworked and underpaid corrections officers were just too easily convinced by a few hundred thousand dollars. He signed the papers that morning and let me walk out with no problems at all. Of course, it would only be a matter of days before they found out I was gone, and by then the Warden would be far away on the beaches of Costa Rica with fresh pussy on his lap. That insignificant blip in their system would suddenly now be an escaped prisoner and soon to be named most wanted fugitive. Forger wasn't wrong, I needed to get the fuck out, and fast, but not without finishing off what I started so long ago.

Hiding in the depths of the Bayou was easy. Getting out required some skill. Skill I'd acquired while shipping girls to Russia. It would take some time, but I'd be heading into Moscow in a few days, and Jameson's new toy would be coming with me.

I looked over at Forger. "First state of business. How about you show me the girl."

12

JAMESON

I DON'T KNOW what the fuck attracted me to this woman.

Her brokenness.

Her need to be with someone.

Willow was so different. She was so sweet, so delicate, I didn't feel the need to hurt anyone back then. I was a good man. Loving. Caring. I barely touched her, and when I did it would be soft, gentle caresses that made her sigh in pleasure. She was passionate and so giving of herself.

But Sadie wasn't Willow, and this was not love. This was fucking lust. Pure fucking lust. That was the only way I could explain it. But the way the woman responded to me. How she'd give herself to me. I'd gotten carried away in her, squeezed a little too tightly, fucked her until she'd passed out. And when she did, a complete and utter pleasure coursed through me as I held her up, spewing cum inside of her.

In these past six years, I'd become a twisted fuck. I was full of rage and anger. But now this woman came into my life and I didn't know what to do with her.

If I let her out of the cage, will she run away from me?

Then again, do I want her to?

She was given to me as a test. What I did with her would allow Petros and the rest of the Royal Bastards to see that I was loyal, that I would take on anything they'd throw at me. But fuck if I didn't want to keep the woman. She was driving me up the wall, insane.

I should be planning out how to get to Rancid, instead. my tongue was down her throat and my dick wet as fuck in that sweet little pussy of hers. Thinking of her now had me adjusting myself in the middle of a Church meeting.

That's how much she'd gotten into my head. I couldn't even fucking remember what the fuck we were talking about. Bullet was giving me the rundown on what the club had been up to money-wise. Didn't look like we had much. Rancid was dealing with the Russians, but not a penny of that was seen in the club. Snake had enlightened us on exactly how he was doing it and it seemed like he had one helluva human trafficking ring set up. I fucking hated that he'd used the club name to do his filthy work. We knew now of his treachery, we just needed to start from zero and find another means to an end.

"Turns out Heavy's got some serious plans on those porn films. He's been traveling all over, I think we should weigh in on it. Looks like good money."

I nodded, in agreement. "All those in favor?"

All of them raised their hands and the next item was brought to the table. "We heard Coy needs some help back in Kentucky."

"How's that?"

"He contacted Rancid a while back saying he needed weapons. BP up in Alaska offered to send what they needed, but they're in need of a transport."

"Why are they hoarding that many firearms?

"Looks like the Bloody Scorpions are wanting to start a war."

I leaned in, elbows on the table and looked around at each

of them while the wheels started spinning. "Bullet, Snake had mentioned a pilot connected to Rancid's whole plan, do you remember his name?"

He nodded. "I remember him. He called himself Bandit. A complete fucking walking disaster."

"Did you find out where he was at?"

"Sure did. Just a few miles away from here. Has his own ranch, and get this. He owns a private airfield."

"Well, fuck me. I think we should pay a visit to this so-called Bandit. Don't you?"

Styx smiled, quickly knowing where I was going with this. "Bullet, make a note, we're gonna be dealing with weapons from now on. Make sure to call Coy and let him know we'll get the shipments out to him. And make sure BP is in the loop. Whatever he's got to transport to Coy, we'll transport it from Seattle. I'll make a call out to F.O.C.U.S. and see what damage can be done on the Iron Pipeline up in New York."

I smiled, for the first time in a long time feeling like I was actually a part of something worth doing. "Looks like we're about to make some bank, Brothers."

They all cheered and banged on the table, seeming excited about our new endeavors. I focused on Tick Tock at the other end of the table. He was our Road Captain and planned everything out for shipments and the such.

"I'm counting on you, TIck Tock, to get shit rollin'. We'll start working on flight plans and routes to make these shipments work. Colt!"

Colt slowly stepped forward. "Gimme the information on all our properties."

"We've got mostly boats, they run along the Bayou and out into the Mississippi. We've got the River's Edge Bar up in town, Tattoo shops in the historic district, and a few pawn shops strewn around town, but they're not makin' us any money."

"We got weapons in those pawn shops?"

He nodded. "Yeah, we keep 'em in storage. Some we take for ourselves."

"You ever heard of straw purchasing."

Colt nodded. "We buy the goods legally, erase the serial numbers and bam."

"Bingo. Only this time, we collect and buy, we don't register them. We peel the serial numbers and we're golden. We keep twenty-five percent of what arrives on the log, the rest we ship."

"I've got a few contacts in Chicago who can help us out with this."

"Then we're about to start a business, Gentlemen."

I smiled at Colt and he nodded at me. He didn't have to say it, he was impressed. We were finally going to start up again and make some decent money doing so. Rancid had driven us to the ground. The only reason this place was standing was because of the money I inherited from my father. The fucker had been stealing it this entire time. He'd liquidated half the account, a quarter of a million dollars gone, just like that. I was livid. Forger, the weasel, had escaped when we dragged Snake out, but as soon as I was able to get my hands on him, I'd make him into another example of what happens when you double-cross me.

I looked over at Knuckles. "Now let's pay this motherfucker a visit."

***

BARRY REED WAS DEFINITELY NOT PREPARED TO HAVE THE ROYAL Bastards barge into his trailer home unannounced. I kicked a beer can out of the way and stepped aside as a half-naked girl ran out, her tits bouncing all over the place. From the backroom, the infamous Bandit stepped out in his dirty underwear.

I grimaced and scratched his stomach as he swept past me.

He bent down and checked each of the empty beer cans that were strewn around the mobile home, and finally found one he could take some leftover drops from.

"This is the Bandit?" I looked at Styx, and he simply shrugged. He was just as confused as I was.

"Look, I already told you, fellas, I don't transport girls anymore. FBI's been crawlin' around here and I'm not in the mood to find myself behind bars."

He had a thick Louisiana accent and from what I could tell, he wasn't very interested in following Rancid's orders anymore.

"I didn't come here to piggyback on the shit Rancid had goin' on. Those dealings are over with Rancid, and my men and I have nothing to do with that. I've come with another offer on the table."

He downed the can and then looked into the dark hole, probably expecting more to magically appear. He flung the empty can into the sink and turned to me. His eyes widened as he realized we weren't who he thought we were. "You ain't Rancid."

"Damn straight I'm not Rancid."

He eyed me for a second and then smirked. "But you're the President of the Royal Bastards."

"That's right."

Slowly, a smile spread on his face. " Well, I'll be damned. You look just like your father. Elrik Jameson, I presume."

I frowned, a bit shocked that he knew my name.

"I have to say it's a pleasure to meet your acquaintance."

"Yeah, well, I can't say the same."

"Your Daddy was a good friend of mine. Got me out of some binds, he did. Sad day, the day he left this earth."

I was surprised that he knew my father. Then again, Bulldog made it a point to know everyone. He'd piqued my curiosity, but I'd ask him about those memories later. Now was the time for business not small talk.

"How did you start working for Rancid?"

He chuckled and walked over to the couch. Plopping himself down, robe opened and underwear showin' shit we didn't want to see. I looked over at Knuckles, but he simply shook his head in amusement.

"I wasn't workin' for Rancid. He was workin' with me. The Russian Bratva had a bounty on my head and Rancid took advantage of that. I was being tag teamed by Rancid and the Russians. He'd find the girls and bring them to me, I'd transport them. Whatever the fee, we split fifty-fifty."

"So that's how he got into this."

Bandit nodded. "I needed the help. He knew how to get the goods. Made the Russians happy, and my neck wasn't on the line anymore. Go figure, Rancid goin' to jail would finally make them stop houndin' me."

"So you're tellin' me you worked with him but never saw his face."

"Not once. He'd have someone drop the girls off late at night. What was his name?"

"Snake," Knuckles pitched in.

"Yep. That was him. He was the one who traveled back and forth with me. Barely said a word, he was in charge of makin' sure they didn't wake up."

"So they were drugged."

"For the most part. Yeah."

I sat down on the edge of the couch and propped my hands on my knees, I turned to him. "I've got a new proposition for you. Something a bit easier. Something that will probably get you out of this shit hole and into something a little more high end."

He leaned forward and I grimaced. The sight of the man's sagging balls was not a welcome one. "I'm listenin'."

"We're looking into gun running."

He whistled and leaned back again, propping his lanky

arms along the top of the couch. "You got heavy ones if you're going that route. I heard the Bloody Scorpions handle shipments round here."

"Don't you worry about them. Only men who run the Mississippi are the Royal Bastards. Besides, we don't want the river this time," I pointed up. "We want the sky."

Bandit smirked. "So what's in it for me?"

"You get twenty percent of the cut."

"Ha! Fuck that! I was making fifty with Rancid."

I looked over at Knuckles and he signaled for me to up the take. "Thirty and that's my final offer. You'll be making twice as much, I guarantee it."

Bandit contemplated it for a few minutes and then looked around his place. "Throw in one of those new mobile homes and I'm in."

"Deal." I reached out my hand and he shook it.

We officially had our pilot and things seemed to be flowing smoothly. I'd leave this in Knuckles' hands and I'd focus on what I came here to do. Enough time wasted on pussy and business. I had other matters I needed to deal with.

❦ 13 ❦

RANCID

"Well, well. Looky what we've got here."

I crouched down by her cot, staring down at the sleeping beauty. "Petros always did have good taste in women."

The woman was sound asleep. Had no clue who'd just entered her world. I reached in through the bars and stroked her cheek. She stirred, and slowly, her eyes fluttered open. When they met mine, they widened, and the sleeping beauty was now just how I needed her.

Wide awake.

Curling up in the cot she watched me beneath hooded lashes. I walked around the room, lightly swinging the blades that had been left hanging.

"Looks like they've taken some of my favorite toys. What a shame. I sure did want to use some of them on you."

I gave her a hard stare and of course, she cowered, avoiding my gaze "Do you know who I am?"

"You're Rancid."

"Ohhh, yes! I do love when women say my name, I especially enjoy when they say it while they beg. Will you beg for me, Sadie?"

She didn't answer and I gripped her hair though the bars and slammed her head back against them. "I said will you beg!"

Her lips quivered and a small yes trembled out. I released her head and she scurried to the center of the cell as if that would protect her. I signaled to Forger to pop open the cell door and he aimed his gun at the lock. She jumped and screamed as he pulled the trigger and the door blew inward.

I slowly made my way into the cell and she immediately tried to run. As she swept past me, I grabbed her hands and swung her around, smashing them together. She whimpered, and smiling down at her, I squeezed tightly. Her scream pierced the silence as I heard her bone snap, her hand breaking.

I let her go and she fell limply to the floor, delicately holding her left hand to her chest. She whimpered, but no tear slid down her cheeks, and I kicked at her. She tried shifting away, but I grabbed her hair and yanked her face up to mine. "I heard you're just as traitorous as your new boyfriend. I so wish Petros would have sent you to me a lot sooner, this tight little pussy would have been mine a long time ago.

"Fuck you."

I laughed and turned to Forger who followed suit. "Fuck, me?"

I turned back to her, menace in my tone. "Fuck. Me? I don't think so, Sleeping Beauty. But I damn sure will be fucking you, just as I did with his other woman. I'd tied her up to the bed, her sweet ass up in the air, her screams piercing the night made me so fuckin' hard for that little girl."

I yanked her head back as I spoke, forcing her eyes on me. "I even enjoyed the gurgling sound of her blood as I slit her throat. Fuck, her pussy tightened up so beautifully when I did that. Swallowing every drop of my cum. Are you gonna do that for me, Sadie? Tighten up around my cock?"

She spit at me and snarled. "Never."

"Vicious kitty. I wonder how vicious you'll be when I have you tied to a post and whip your ass."

"Jameson is going to rip you apart."

I laughed. "I can't contain my excitement as I patiently wait to see him try."

I stroked a piece of a golden lock that fell over her pretty eyes, and I got lost in thought of what I'd done so long ago. "Last time I took what was his, he sobbed like a little baby. I wonder. If I take his brand new toy. Will he sob just as much?"

My eyes met hers and I could see her visibly trembling, but she held my gaze, and I could see the anger flooding through her. She hadn't even shed one tear when I broke her hand and I was curious...

I gingerly tugged on her arm and she shook her head, fear engulfing her eyes. I tsked and cooed as I lifted her broken wrist. As my eyes met hers I lifted her hand back, hearing the snap of her already broken bones. She screamed and slumping forward into my arms, she shook, but she didn't let out one tear.

"Fascinating," I pushed her hair back and lifted her chin so she'd look at me. "Pain sluts are my favorite."

I signaled for Forger to take her and bandage up her wrist before making sure she was chained and locked up for my enjoyment. He gagged her right before flinging her over his left shoulder, she spat curses at me as she was carried away.

I looked around the cell and smiled. I'd kept such succulent pussy in these confines, all ready for me to use and abuse. My secrets had remained well hidden for years. But I'd once again get my fill soon enough. All I needed was to get to Bandit and we'd be flying out without any problems at all. But first...first, I wanted to have a little fun.

***

WE'D TAKEN HER BACK TO THE CABIN. I WANTED TO KEEP HER intact but had to ruin her pretty face as I shoved a rifle into it to keep her from screaming any further. She was out cold as we dragged her inside and hung her up to the rafters in the center of the cabin. We'd stripped her bare and I waited until she'd wake. I dragged a chair out and got comfortable. I lit up a cigar and took a few puffs staring at her. Her face was a bloodied mess, her golden locks now limp strands that stuck to her forehead from the humidity. She stirred and then screamed awake as her broken wrist was tugged on by the chains. A sob finally escaped her, but no tears.

I circled her naked form, tracing her bare skin. Her tits trembled as her nipples puckered up, and the sound of the chains shaking made me rock hard. "You're resolute, aren't you? Barely giving me a tear."

I brushed the hair from her face and lifted her chin. She flinched from the movement but held my gaze, that fierce look making me chuckle. I was going to enjoy breaking her. I puffed thick smoke into her face and the look of disgust she gave me only urged me on even more.

I swept down and lifted the hot iron from the burning fireplace. I lifted it up near her face and let her see the symbol of the letter R. "I got this especially for you, sweet girl. Let's see if we can make those tears fall."

I pressed the iron into her smooth flesh, right above her groin. She gave out a strangled scream and began to convulse on the chains. Right as the scent of her flesh reached her nostrils, she passed out once again. I shook my head, throwing the hot iron back into the flames.

"Not as strong as I thought you'd be."

Her flesh was red and sore as I traced it. My mark etched onto her skin forever. If he ever again got the chance to look at it, he'd remember my name. Taking out my phone, I took a few shots. Close-ups of her bruised face, her broken hand, and that beautiful branding I had just given her. The rest of the shots were of her naked form, limp and swinging from the chains. When I was done I sent it out to the one person I knew would get the message across.

I sat back down on the chair in front of her and took a puff of my cigar feeling more than satisfied. It was only a matter of time, but I'd make sure he'd never see her again.

❧ 14 ❧

JAMESON

HEADING up the path to the metal barn, I had finally decided I was going to let Sadie go. I couldn't keep her locked up in here forever, and I was done being a pawn in Petros' games. I was the goddamn National Chapter President. He wanted my loyalty, then he'd have to prove his first.

Who the fuck did he think he was anyway?

I tore open the shed door and the air got sucked out of me. The cell was empty. I moved in cautiously, wary of my surroundings. I could sense the evilness that remained. She didn't escape, she was taken.

As I proceeded to walk in further, I noticed the piece of paper jammed into one of the hanging hooks. I tore it off and read the uneven script.

Finders. Keepers.
You take what's mine and I take what's yours.
Let's see if this one survives.

"Motherfucker," I crumbled the note in my fist, rage completely consuming me.

I stormed back into the clubhouse, and Colt was the first person I came across. I must have looked like a mad man because he stopped in his tracks.

"He took her," my voice was low and uneven.

"What are you talking about?"

I shoved the piece of paper into his chest and yelled out. "He fucking took her!"

Colt took a moment to read the note and then signaled for Church. I grabbed the lapels of his jacket and he did the same to mine.

"I am going to destroy him." My voice shook as I spoke.

"And I've got your back, Brother."

I looked up at him and the look he gave me told me that he understood exactly where I was coming from. He'd seen me like this before, when I found out about Willow. He was the only person, other than Rael, who had understood the help-lessness in my eyes. The members started to gather around and I let Colt take the lead.

"We need to scour the nearby hunting grounds. Rancid took Sadie. We don't know when, but it had to have been some time between noon and now, which means he's not that far away."

"And if you find him," I seethed. "You bring him to me."

A collective, Yes Prez, resounded as everyone moved into action. "This is gonna be like finding a needle in a haystack."

Colt grunted. "Rancid ain't that smart. He's close. I can tell you that. He's the type who likes to watch his victims suffer. And I'm sorry Brother, but you are one of those victims he enjoys to torture."

"I won't lose her, Colt. I can't."

We'll find her, Brother."

I gripped onto his jacket and shook my head. "She means something to me. Do you understand me?"

He gripped me by the shoulder and spoke low. "We will find her. And she'll be in one piece. Come on, I'll ride with you."

He turned to Knuckles and Styx and made sure they were following me as well. Wherever he was keeping her, I was going to save her. I couldn't let what happened to Willow happen to Sadie. This time around, I wouldn't be able to live with myself.

The bikes rolled out onto the old dirt roads. The sun had gone down and we were engulfed in the darkness of the Bayou. I didn't find comfort in this darkness, instead, a heavy eeriness surrounded us as the sounds of frogs and crickets filled the night. As we turned onto another road, the old LA57 sign came into view. I turned to Colt, but he kept his eyes locked on the road.

One didn't take LA57 so lightly, and I could sense that I wasn't the only one who had just gone on full alert. I could feel the hairs stand in the back of my neck. An ominous sensation overcame me and I gripped the handles on the bike and kept my focus on the deep twists and turns of the old highway. Adelaine's words echoed in my head.

Take care where your path leads you. Veer away from evil and into the light.

None of us went down this road on purpose. One of the most haunted roads in Louisiana and it sat on Indigenous burial grounds. The fucker lived in the middle of nowhere, and Colt seemed to know exactly where he was going. He suddenly swerved off the road and deeper into the swamps. We followed him and I could feel the edginess in the air. This was spiritual grounds and we had no business traveling through it.

Styx's bike swerved slightly left and he managed to straighten it, lifting his hand to signal he was alright. After what seemed like a fucking eternity, Colt turned his lights off and we let the bikes glide up to an old ratchety looking camping cabin. The place was nearly falling apart, the screen door swung off its hinges, the wood splintered, and the staircase leading up to the front door had holes in it.

Warily, I got off my bike and we gathered off towards the back of the cabin. "How do you know this is the place?"

"Because he brought me here once. Right after the clubhouse burnt down. We were doing a job and he got shot by the Bloody Scorpions. The closest place we could hide was out in the swamps and that's when he told me about the cabin."

The lights were on inside but the place was eerily quiet. The sounds that filled the Bayou were non-existent along these parts, and that feeling of being watched was continuous. I pulled out my gun and left it at my side. The weight of it brought comfort.

"Styx and Knuckles you take the back, Colt and I will take the front. Riddick, Tick Tock, and Bullet you stay put, anything happens to us you know what to do. And if you get your hands on Rancid, you keep that motherfucker alive."

They all nodded and slowly crept into the treeline, guns aimed high, forming a defense line. Knuckles and Styx disappeared towards the back of the cabin while Colt and I slowly made our way to the front door. I wanted this to be done as quickly as possible. We stepped up, one on either side of the door. The screen door was in our way, and I slowly pulled it towards me. It screeched loudly and I looked over at Colt who instantly moved into action. I ripped the door off its hinges and Colt kicked his way in. We moved stealthily through the house, clearing each room and making sure no surprises were waiting for us. We met up with Styx and Knuckles in the hallway and they shook their heads letting me know there was nothing. The fucking cabin was empty.

In the heavy silence, Knuckles' cell phone suddenly pinged and as he looked down at his phone, his expression darkened. When his eyes met mine I knew something was up.

"What is it?"

"I don't think you should…"

I reached for the phone and yanked it out of his hand before he could protest. I looked over the messages and then I swept through them once again. She was bound and naked right here in this fucking cabin. I walked over to the fireplace and leaning forward I lifted the hot iron. I gripped it tightly in my fist, hatred running through me.

"Jameson," Knuckles spoke, but I held my hand up to stop him. I didn't want to hear anything else. I stared down at the phone and stared at her beautiful body dangling so obscenely.

"If he hurts her, I'm going to make sure he's alive long enough to have each limb torn from his body and fed to the fucking gators."

My phone rang at that moment and Bandit's name flashed across the phone screen. I let it ring for a second, but I had this off feeling I needed to answer it.

"Talk."

"I think you need to get your asses down here."

I signaled to Colt and turned the phone on speaker as they all stepped up to listen. "What's going on?"

"Rancid stopped in, left me a little present."

I took off, out the door and down the steps, calling orders. Pressing the phone to my ear I continued my conversation. "Is she alive?"

"She's breathing. They knocked her out before they got here. Forger is outside, he won't leave her side."

"Where is Rancid going?"

"Out to Seattle. He's taking the same route to get himself out as he did the rest of the girls."

"When did he say he'd be back?"

"He said he had to run an errand, that was fifteen minutes ago. This was my only chance to call you."

"We'll be there in ten. Stall him. And Bandit…"

"Yeah."

"Thank you."

Starting up the bikes, we took off. As we sped through those haunting twisted roads my sole focus was on getting there as fast as possible. I wasn't going to lose Sadie. I couldn't lose her. Her bright blue eyes crossed my mind and I slowly realized what Adelaine Laveaux meant by following the light. She was it, that light. And as much as I was trying to justify it, she meant more to me than I thought. I never promised her anything, never spoke of feelings or futures together, but I didn't want her gone. She was sent to me for a reason. Whether it was to lead me towards my path of vengeance, or it was to guide me out, I needed her.

Sadie Forrester belonged to me.

❧ 15 ❧

SADIE

MY HEAD POUNDED as I came to. I blinked a few times until the blurriness went away and then I lay there, staring up at an old ceiling fan which was slowly turning, a failed attempt to provide any type of coolness. The humidity was toxic in Louisiana, you could barely breathe, and tonight it felt like a ton of bricks on my chest. When I tried to move, I flinched, noticing my hand had been bandaged and put in a splint. I groaned from the pain.

"Oh, careful there."

A man I hadn't seen before came up to me and helped me into a seated position. "Wh-who are you?"

He smiled at me and looked behind him to where that other man, the one called Forger, was sitting watching TV in the room adjacent. The man placed a finger to his lips and winked at me.

"Name's Barry. Barry Reed. But most folk call me Bandit."

"What is this place?" Even my voice sounded weak and everything hurt. I hissed as I shifted, a sharp pain shooting across my groin. I quickly lifted my shirt and tugged down the waistband of my pants to see the branding that was left on me.

"Fuck, that looks like it hurt."

I held back the tears that were threatening to consume me. "It did."

"I'll get you somethin' for that."

He scrambled through a first aid kit and came back with three items. Whiskey, ointment, and gauze. "Take a swig of this."

"Gladly," I grabbed the bottle and took long pulls.

He chuckled and grabbed it from me. "Easy there, I do need it. Bite down on this. He gave me a rag and I did as he asked. Then he poured the whiskey across the burn mark and I jolted nearly doubling over in pain.

"Fuck," he cursed as he cleaned me up, then placed ointment and the gauze over the wound. "I can't say it's not going to scar."

"I know."

I watched him as he crossed the room towards a small fridge and grabbed a bottle of water and then handed me four aspirins to go along with it. "Take 'em, you'll need them."

Gratefully, I downed them, and then stared up at him. "You're not one of them."

"No way in hell."

He took a quick look back at Forger and then crouched down before me. "But help is on its way," he assured me and my eyes widened. "Just stay put."

I nodded as he walked towards Forger, sitting down beside him. He chuckled at whatever was on the TV, but as he leaned back in the chair he looked over at me and winked.

Could it be true?

Was this man actually on my side?

Rancid had wanted to destroy me, to truly watch me crumble, but I hadn't given him the satisfaction. The beatings my mother had given me as a child had numbed me to any kind of pain. I'd had broken bones before, none as brutal as what he'd ensued, but horrid enough that I knew what it felt like. The pain ran through me like a memory and I welcomed it. It was the only way not to let it consume me. I had no heroes in my life, so it was difficult for me to believe that help was truly coming. In order for that to happen, it meant that I was important to Jameson. And as much as I hoped that was true, my life was filled with disappointment, and the knowledge that the only one who could help me...was me.

The roar of motorcycles arriving was deafening. Bright lights flashed around the trailer home and shook the ground where it stood.

"What the fuck is that?!"

Forger stood up, his gun out as he looked through the blinds. "Fuck. Me!"

He turned, looking like a madman as he scrounged to find some way to escape, and then his eyes landed on me. "Get the fuck up!"

Grabbing me, he yanked me off the seat and placed me into a chokehold. "I ain't goin' down like this, and your sweet ass is gonna help me get out of this."

"Forger!" Jameson's voice rang loud and clear. "We know you're alone, so I suggest you get your ass out here and hand over the girl."

"Fuck. Fuuuck!" He yanked the door open and shoved me forward. I could make out maybe fifteen bikes. Jameson was up front, his hand held up, stopping the men from shooting at me. Forger forced me out, using me as a human shield.

"Don't force me to put a bullet in her, because I have no problems doing so!"

Jameson smirked, his stance relaxed as he watched everything play out in front of him. As I said, he was methodical and deliberate, and he was giving Forger his moment. One which would be his last.

"How long did you say we had?"

"He'll be here in ten minutes!" Bandit's voice rose from within the mobile home.

"Motherfucker!" Forger screamed, turning the gun behind me and shooting into the trailer home.

"Eh, eh, eh!" Jameson yelled out, his gun pointed at Forger. I looked back at him, his eyes penetrating me with a fierce gaze. He'd come for me. I didn't think he would but he did, and that meant he cared. He cared for my life as much as I cared for him.

"You okay in there!"

"As good as can be!" Bandit responded.

"Put the gun down, Forger, or you're gonna force me to do something I don't want to do."

Forger guffawed. "You're gonna do it anyway, but before you do, I'll take her out first." He aimed the gun to my head and shoved me a few steps forward.

Jameson angled his gun, his eyes on me once again and an unspoken connection was made. He was going to take him out, no matter what. His brow scrunched up in an apologetic look and tears finally fell down my cheeks.

Do it. I mouthed the words to him and he fought with himself for a minute before he finally aimed the gun a bit higher.

"I'm giving you one more chance, Forger!"

I could clearly see he didn't want to do this, but the man behind me wasn't giving him much choice. I tried to think as to how I could get out of his hold, but his arm squeezed me tighter as he moved us over to the right.

"I warn you, Jameson!"

He kept walking us back towards the back of the mobile home. He kept talking about not going out like this, that he wasn't going to die for Rancid. Jameson followed us, gun pointed at his head, waiting for the right moment and then suddenly, a gun fired and

I screamed as the impact shoved me forward. Forger crumbled to the ground and I fell to my knees.

I stayed there, looking at my shaking hands as a cold shiver ran up and down my spine. Jameson ran up to me and he was saying something but in my dumbfoundedness, I couldn't make it out. When Jameson turned I saw a man standing in the shadows.

Jameson trained the gun on him, he pushed me behind his back, still protecting me. I hung onto Jameson's jacket, light-headed and weak. The man slowly stepped out of the shadows and into the light. Jameson froze and then slowly put his gun down.

"Well, I'll be damned. I guess the Devil is on my side."

"He is when I'm around."

The two men embraced, patting themselves on the back as if they were old friends.

"I never thought I'd see your ugly mug again."

Jameson actually laughed, a bright smile that reached his eyes, and all I could think was how handsome he was. Jameson finally turned to me, as I stood there just watching their reunion.

"You alright, Sweetheart?" The man asked me, and suddenly the world dipped from under and I fell. I felt Jameson's arms around and I heard orders being given. I was then handed over to someone, telling them to take me to the hospital.

"I'll be by your side as soon as I can, Sadie." I felt his lips on my forehead and then the darkness engulfed me.

❧ 16 ❧

JAMESON

I LOOKED over at Rael who'd surprised us only minutes before. He'd gotten news that Rancid had gotten out of jail, and had taken a flight down to offer some help. Grim, his Chapter's Prez, had come down with him to offer any backup we may need. Grim was a good man, and he was like family to Rael and Willow. When we were running, he'd taken us in instantly. No questions asked, and I respected him greatly for that. He put his head on the cutting board for us, and he did so every day after that. He protected Ian as much as he could, and I knew if I would have stayed, he would have done the same for me.

"You ready?"

"As ready as I'll ever be."

"When all this is said and done we need to sit down and have a beer. You need to tell me all about that Devil's Ride."

He smirked. "Trust me. You don't want to know about that. It's a lot darker than you think and it eats at your soul."

"But you went through with it?"

He nodded and had this far off look, as if though he were remembering. "Just trust me when I say that if I could change my past, I would."

I looked over at him and I could tell by the look on his face that he'd gone through some shit in the last six years. The ghost of his sister haunted him and I knew he'd been fighting his own battles. There were men who'd sent Rancid out to collect Willow, the same men who Rancid had worked for. They were part of the Russian Bratva, and Rael had been chasing those ghosts for years. When he did catch up with them, they would die a very brutal death at his hands.

The sound of a motorcycle interrupted the silence and signaled that Rancid had finally arrived. Guns out, we took our positions at either side of the door. We looked at each other and nodded.

It was finally time.

***

WE'D SEATED RANCID IN THE CENTER OF THE CELL HE'D USED TO put his victims in. Straps had been secured around his ankles and wrists and a gag placed in his mouth. We hadn't given him a chance. As soon he'd opened that door, we came down on him hard, taking him to his knees and slamming the butt of the gun to the back of his head. He'd instantly crumbled to the floor., Without waiting any further, we tied him up and threw him in the trunk of the cage, deciding to take him back to the metal barn.

I'd ordered the Presidents of the Chapters to come down and join us for Church. The orders were mandatory, and I'd heard they'd started arriving as early as this morning. No one was to go near Rancid. And Knuckles had been on guard all night as I'd gone to visit Sadie and made sure she was alright.

She'd been sedated and the doctors told me they would be

able to repair her wrist. I had asked for a plastic surgeon to look at her mark and he'd assured me he'd do his best to make it disappear. I'd practically threatened him into doing so. My woman wasn't going to suffer looking at that for the rest of her life. She'd already been through enough.

I left her early this morning and came down to finish the job. Rael met me in the cell just as Rancid was waking up. Removing the gag, Rael swatted him on the head and he snarled a *fuck you*.

I stood before him and smirked. "I finally get to see your ugly face."

"Untie me you fucking shit, and have at me man to man."

"Oh, no, no, no, we are so far past that. Don't for one second think I won't put you down like the dog you are, fuck, a dog is more human than you are. No, you deserve special treatment."

I reached my hand out and Rael placed the blow torch into my hand. "Do you remember this?"

He sneered at me, the muscles in his arms bulging from the tension. "Cause I still remember it," I pulled up my sleeve to show him the scar he'd left. Leaning forward, I glared at him, stating the following words.

"You're about to feel the most unbearable pain possible. I sure can't wait to hear you scream."

Lighting up the blow torch, I slowly focused the flame on his arm and proceeded to burn the patch off. The tattoo slowly dissipated as the smell of burnt flesh filled the metal shed. His high pitched screams echoed all around us, and after a few minutes of convulsing in the chair, he slumped over. I cut the flame short and looked down at him.

"Fuck. Me. I really wanted him to last longer." I looked up at Rael. "Wake him up."

Taking a pair of pliers off the wall, he walked over to Rancid and got to one knee before him. He started with his pinky toe first. As soon as he closed the pliers around his toe, the sound of bone-shattering resounded through the nearly empty space. Rancid awoke instantly, a scream lodged in his throat as Rael went ahead and clamped down on the next toe. At this point, Rancid was partially lucid, drool dribbling down his chin. Rael waited another second before taking the third toe. He clamped down on it a little too hard, and it dangled off a bit.

I pressed the back of my hand to my mouth and winced. "Fuck, that had to have hurt."

Rancid was completely knocked out. The pain had been too horrific for him, but it was only fair he suffer the same kind of pain that he inflicted on those children.

Of course, this was nothing compared to what he'd done. He'd held those girls for months. Defiling and raping them over and over again. But in these last few hours, we'd make sure he understood what it meant to suffer.

Taking the bucket of cold water, I slammed it against his face, and he sputtered gasping for air. He raised his head and started to give out an eerie laugh. Fucker was crazier than I thought, and as he began to talk I knew he was looking for his death wish.

"I'll never forget her sweet screams as I fucked her ass. So fucking tight."

I slammed my fist against his jaw and he stopped for a moment, spitting out blood before continuing.

"She cried out your name over and over as she came all over my cock. That's when I forced her to look at herself in the mirror. Tears in those pretty eyes."

I slammed my fist against him again, this time hearing a satisfying crunch as I broke his nose. He looked at me, evilness in that stare.

"That's when I slit her throat while I fucked the life right out of her."

Rael slammed his fist into him that time, a roar emanating from him as Rancid's head fell lifelessly to the side.

"Shut him up!"

Rael did just that, clamping down on his next toe and he bent it this way and that until it snapped. Rancid screamed and wailed, cursing and spitting venom on us, but we ignored him as Rael went from toe to toe, breaking each one. To us he wasn't human, he was shit that needed to be taught a lesson and then disposed of.

"You're gonna pay for this," he seethed.

I laughed and Rael proceeded to remove the straps, "Let's do this. If you can manage to walk out the door, we'll let you go."

Rael and I stood aside and watched as Rancid tried to get up and leave. As soon as his feet hit the concrete he crumbled to his knees with a wait. Then he slowly began to crawl towards the door. We lifted him and placed him face down on a nearby table. Strapping his hands and feet down, we did exactly what he'd done to those girls. Taking a hot tire iron we'd left in burning coal, I placed it by his head and leaned over him.

"This is for all the girls you raped and maimed." Without warning, I shoved iron up his ass. He gave out a long wail as I shoved it in deeper and then he passed out on us.

"Did you kill him?"

"Now what fun would that be," I looked up at Rael and he smirked.

"You're a sick fuck."

"Never said I wasn't."

We were at it for a few more hours, taking a smoke break in between, and then waking him up for another round of torture. Each time we thought we'd be done, he'd say something else to instigate us. He showed no remorse for the crimes he's committed, on the contrary, he proudly re-lived every single one of them, telling us in detail what he'd done to each girl. How he'd tormented and ruined them. And when they were too broken to fuck, he'd cut them up in pieces, tying bricks to their mutilated bodies and sinking them in the Bayou.

Each story only made me want to prolong his torture. I had no pity on him. At one point I set the flame torch to his balls, and as the smell of burning flesh began to hit our nostrils he finally begged us to let him go. That he would never do it again. That he was *sorry*.

We both laughed at his attempt to show any remorse. "There's no forgiveness here, Motherfucker!"

Grabbing the crowbar, I slammed it against his face and with a grunt, he collapsed.

Rael stood quietly to the side, "We'll leave him there until everyone arrives."

As I walked out, he stopped me. "What are you thinking of doing?"

I looked back at the piece of shit on the table. "I think everyone deserves a piece of him."

"Are you satisfied with all this?"

I looked down at the ground and shook my head. "I find no satisfaction in this. I'm just seeking justice for those he hurt."

"Willow deserves justice to be made."

"Willow deserves a lot more than justice. She deserves so much more, and I let her down."

"You can't blame yourself."

"But I do. I should have been there. To protect her. And I should have removed this threat when I had the chance."

"I don't blame you, and neither should you. What happened was not your fault. It was his." He pointed at Rancid who lay limp on the table. "You wanna take it out on someone, you take it out on that motherfucker."

I stared up at him and nodded. "I'm not done with him yet. Come on, the show's just about to get good."

❦ 17 ❧

JAMESON

WHEN I CALLED Church yesterday I didn't expect everyone to show so quickly. I had every President of all twenty-six chapters come down to see the spectacle. It was only fair. They all had their reservations on Rancid. Some openly showed their disdain such as F.O.C.U.S. and Rael, and then there were those who quietly waited in the background for their turn to come.

And they would all get their turn.

I took my time walking down the steps and into the foyer, all eyes were on me as I looked around the room. Koyn stood to my right, the President of the Oklahoma Chapter wore his scars proudly, showing the pain he'd endured. You had to respect him for that. Capone and Blayze from the L.A. Chapter stood next to him. I met Capone's gaze and I could tell he was just waiting for the moment that I'd give him the green light to take his fury out n Rancid. Dog had been a friend, and someone he respected. He'd been wanting to get a piece of Rancid for some time now, and although he didn't know it, today he'd have his chance. Then there was Animal, Alec Walker. Loyal as fuck and took shit from nobody. I nodded at him as I passed by. And then I paused when I came to Heavy. He lowered his head as I stepped up to him. Heavy was the Washington, D.C. Chapter President. He was into pussy and porn, but I knew he wasn't into beating or killing women. I didn't have to say it, he damn well knew he did wrong by Gamble, but according to Colt, he hated Rancid as much as the rest of us. He looked up at me and there was an understanding there. What was done to Gamble was wrong and that was enough for me.

Hatch and Hype had come in from Miami. Hype's business seemed to be flowing smoothly until recently, so I made a mental note to talk to him later about it. He needed to put a strong arm on that new Chief of Police and get the goods across one way or another. The Royal Bastards always found a way to get what we wanted and I was willing to give him a hand.

Nycto stood in the shadows, he was dressed in black leather, sunglasses hid his face. He always did have a thing for darkness. Twisted motherfucker walled people up for a living, some dark mojo existed there. Especially when you could hear the moans of the condemned through the walls. He fucking creeped me out, and I was glad he was on my side and that I had his respect. I nodded at him in greeting as I passed by. He and I had a conversation pending over how to handle shipments correctly. We transferred goods, we didn't ask questions, nor did we become fucking heroes. You don't dip into what you transport, but apparently, Nycto forgot that along the way. There was more to his story than he let on, and eventually, I'd get the truth out of him.

Savage was the Prezsidentover in Alabama. He sat in the far back, looking stoic and eerily quiet. It seemed that whatever was going on with the Dragons, a rival gang, was weighing him down. He'd ridden down with two people, Bowie and Dallas. I was surprised since he usually kept to himself and he damn well knew that women and civilians stayed out of club business. If he brought them down with him it was because he was protecting them, and the look in his eyes told me he had somethin' on his mind. I had questions, but my main concern was what type of implications these fucking Dragons could bring onto the club. If my brother needed backup, I'd make it known.

Barracuda from Sacramento stopped me for a minute to welcome me back, and King and Duke from Santa Clarita, California nodded to me in greeting. They all seemed friendly enough and pretty relaxed as I walked around the room.

Voodoo nodded to me as I walked by. He always knew my moods and I always knew his. It was like that for as long as I could remember. I gave him a pat on the back, glad to see him again. Venom stood at his side and I reached out and shook his hand.

"Got talking to your grandmother the other night."

"So I heard."

"She's a tough cookie."

That made him smile. "You don't know the half of it."

Voodoo arched a brow. "Guess Rancid didn't have his way after all?"

I gave him half a smile. "Did you ever think he would?"

"I knew you were lying in wait. It was a matter of time."

As I turned around, Petros was eyeing me. "You want to tell me why she's still alive."

I smiled as I stared down at the floorboards. "This ain't the time to have this conversation."

"So you're just going to accept that there's a traitor among us."

He was instigating a fight and I wasn't having that. Not today. "I'm not here to issue punishments at your command just because your precious ego got hurt. Get over it."

"She's a fucking whore."

I grabbed him by the lapels of his jacket and he fisted mine. It took all my control not to slam my fist into his face. He was pushing me. "I suggest you watch your words."

He narrowed his eyes on me and then realization made

them go wide. "I should have known Hart wasn't the only man she'd go after."

"Goddammit, Petros! I'm done with these bullshit games. I'm claiming Sadie Forrester." I turned to the rest of the room. "Does anybody have a problem with that?"

A collective, *No Sir*, resounded and I closed in on Petros, speaking low so only he could hear me. "I don't want any problems, but I also won't let you continue to test my loyalty. I'm as loyal as they come and you damn well know it."

He smirked and shook his head. "All I have to say is don't come crying to me when she fucks around on you. I warned you."

Petros and I would never see eye to eye, but either way, he was still an appointed President and whether he liked it or not, we had to respect each other. "She's no longer your business."

As I moved to the center of the room I came across Coy. I'd called him up with specific instructions, and he was more than willing to help me out. I couldn't have the FBI sniffin' around here and finding corpses. Because that's exactly how Rancid was going to leave this place. As a fucking corpse. There was only one person I thought of who I could count on, and Coy was that person.

"Did you bring it?"

"Yup, it's out back."

"So I can count on you after we're all done here."

"We'll take him back to the crematorium, no one's gonna ask us any questions. We'll burn the fucker until he's ash, maybe even mix him in some pig shit. Ain't gonna be any traces of him after we're done with him."

"Perfect. That's exactly what I want to hear."

I moved on to the center of the Foyer and all eyes were on me. "It's good to see you all."

"Good to have you back," Voodoo shouted from the back and there were nods and murmurs of agreement all around.

"I'm pretty sure you all found out I was back a few weeks ago. The reason I called you all down here is that as you know, there was some unfinished business I needed to take care of. I figured you'd all want to know what was going down. And I think you'll appreciate what we have in store for you all."

I stayed quiet for a long moment before continuing. From my right, Colt and Knuckles entered the room, waiting on my signal.

"There's someone I want you all to give a greeting to. But this won't be any normal greeting. Every single one of you will have a chance to express exactly what you think of this person. But I warn you, his last breath is mine."

I signaled to Knuckles and he disappeared through a set of doors. I remained quiet, staring at the ground as he was brought in, screaming obscenities and wailing in pain as his broken toes were being dragged along the floorboards. Rael and Knuckles dumped him in the center of the room and left him there for everyone to take in the monster that was Rancid.

Yanking him by his hair, I hoisted him up so everyone could have a look at him. The room was dead silent.

"Look around you, *Brother*. You have visitors."

He looked up at me and spit flew into my face. I gave him a menacing smile, swiping it away. "Take care of him."

They all knew what I meant by it. It was a trademark I carried with me since I'd been a Sargent At Arms. One he'd used on me before. This type of punishment would always be bestowed on someone who betrayed us.

One after the other, their billie clubs drawn as they came up and had their turn on him. Rancid had no choice as one by one, the Presidents of the Royal Bastards MC took their fury out on him. Years of turmoil, injustices, and unnecessary deaths because of him. They had been at his mercy for too long, and this was justice for all of them. Blayze was furious, thwacking him right on his already bruised ribs. He rolled up into a hunched position only to be brought down by Mammoth, Gamble's right-hand man. Ravage came in next, and he swiped him on his knees. Blood ran down his face and I crouched down before him, wiping it away from his eyes.

"How ya doin', Rancid? You need a break."

"Fuck you!"

"Alright then," I backed away, raising my hands and allowing the punishment to continue. "Just don't want you bleeding out on me before all the fun starts."

His wail of agony ran through me and I smiled, pleased, as I watched from the shadows. One by one the members of the Baltimore Chapter came up and had their share of the fun. Dog had been their President and he had been a good man. They had every right to partake in Rancid's punishment.

I called it when I saw Rancid spewing blood. He was barely breathing at that point. I placed a chair in the center of the Foyer and Knuckles and Rael dragged him onto the seat. He was wheezing as blood seeped from his nose, his eye practically bulging out.

"How does it feel to be on the receiving end of the punishment, Rancid?"

"Fuck. You." He seethed, blood and drool dribbling down his chin, and I grimaced in disgust.

"Penance doesn't come easy for you, does it? Pain. Now pain, that's penance. Are you ready for some pain, Rancid?"

I smacked his cheek in amusement as the rope was dragged across his wrists and ankles, tying him to the chair and holding him steady for what was to come next. Every struggle made him whine and flinch in pain, and I smiled knowing what was to come.

The sound of a motorcycle engine signaled her arrival. She was to get there at this exact time, not a minute too early. Stepping away from the piece of shit in the middle of the floor, I'd left the best for last. Ravage and Mammoth opened the double doors as she walked up the steps. Cautiously, she made her way in, the cute little thing she was. Tiny yet ferocious. And she took no shit from anybody. Warily, she looked at me as I stood in her way, blocking her view.

"Jameson?"

"It's good to see you, Gamble."

She looked back at the man who'd walked in with her. "This must be Hart."

I saw a movement from my peripheral and I turned to look at Petros. "This is not the time."

"It's good to have you back, Prez."

"Do you know why you're here?"

"Not really. Last time I was here I was raped and my lover was murdered, so let's just say it doesn't bring back the best of memories."

"You and I, Gamble. We're a lot alike."

"Oh?"

"More than you think."

She looked up at me, a fierce look in her eye. " Look, Prez, if you called me here to strip me of my title..." she paused, and once again looked back at Hart, but continued to ramble on. "I mean I know you don't think I'm not cut out for this shit, and to have a woman, I mean..but..."

I held my hand up, cutting her off. "You have shown that you can do this, and you have the armor to back you up." I looked over at the three men who hovered around her. Mammoth, Ravage and Hart stared back at me, uncertainty in their eyes.

"No one's gonna hurt you anymore, Gamble."

She looked up at me, bright eyes that held a lot of pain and suffering. I stepped back and swiped my hand across so she could see what I had in store for her. "I called you here because I need you to help me finish a job."

Her hands came up to cover her lips, her eyes wide in

shock. "I think Dog would appreciate this," I whispered to her as she slowly stepped up to the chair.

"Rancid?"

His left eye was sealed shut, his right, barely opened. "You called *her* to finish me off?" His voice was hoarse, and he chuckled sarcastically, coughing up blood and spitting it down at her feet. "She's a worthless whore. She ain't got the balls for it."

I reached out and pressed my blade into her hand. Her eyes met mine and the look in them spoke of true gratefulness. Taking the blade, she closed her finger around in and grasped onto it tightly.

"You know what to do."

She slowly stepped up to him, dragging her fingers through his hair, she tugged his head back, and he dared to smile up at her. Bloodstained his teeth and a busted lip caused him to snarl nastily.

"I've lived my entire life to see this day. I've watched everything crumble before my eyes. I even thought about killing myself after what you did to my family. But there was only one thing that kept me alive all this time. That kept me from putting a gun to my head. I kept telling myself that karma would work itself around in the end, and now it's so fucking glorious that it's finally here."

She leaned down and pressed her cheek to his. "This one's for Dog," her voice held conviction, and as she held his head still, my blade slid across his throat, in one deadly sweep.

There was a heavy silence that fell upon us. The only sound was that of him choking on his own blood. She stepped away, the blade clattering onto the floor, and Hart came up behind her, placing his hands on her shoulders in comfort.

I walked up to him, the hot iron he'd used on Sadie was now burning in my hand. He struggled in the chair for air as I watched him, waiting patiently for his life to seep away.

Willow's innocent face came to my mind, her beautiful smile, how full of life she'd been.

They say vengeance is not the answer, but what is true is that it's a dish best served cold, and mine tasted fucking delicious.

As his eyes met mine, I could see how his soul struggled, a look of true fear in his eyes. It satisfied me to know, I was the last person he'd see before the devil dragged his soul into the depths of hell. I lifted the iron, and his eyes opened wide as I slammed it onto his forehead, branding him just like he had Sadie. His head flew back and his body tumbled to the floor. It convulsed for a few seconds before he went still, the smell of burnt flesh filled the air and a few of the men gagged. We all stood there in a circle, staring down at him. Coy moved first, dragging him up and getting his prospects to take him out back to the horse trailer he'd brought in.

Vengeance had finally taken its reward and as Gamble and I stared at one another I knew it was beyond justified.

ROYAL BASTARDS MC

EPILOGUE

JAMESON

One month later...

Her pussy wrapped and pulsed around my cock as she lifted her hips and seated me inside of her. Her wrists were cuffed to the bed frame as I fucked her. She'd been playing with me all day, eager kitty begging for me to take her. She liked to be forced, to be played with, a pain slut all around. I loved seeing the lash of a whip curl along her flesh, and I cherished each moan and greedy sigh as my crop would leave welts on her pale white flesh. She gripped my cock so good with each spank and bite, and I lived to create that pain for her.

I grinded into her, our body meeting halfway, the pleasure coursing through us both. Reaching up, I turned the key on the cuffs and she quickly slid out of them and I entwined my fingers with her, holding her still as I drove inside of her. Deep thrusts that made her squeal. I leaned in and bit down on her earlobe.

"Needy cunt."

"Yes," she hissed as I fucked her like she'd begged me to.

I finally had her cumming, the tightening of her body beneath me and those sinful moans were music to my ears. It didn't take much to make her orgasm. Sometimes only a matter of seconds, the best was when she'd come as soon as I slid inside of her because I knew the fun was just beginning. A game to see just how much pleasure I could give her.

In the last month, she'd been recuperating, and I'd been gentle with her. Caring that I didn't hurt her too much. But today had been the tipping point. Today I'd taken my fill of her, and as I dipped my cock into her wetness, and held her pinned down to the mattress, her mewls of pleasure only fueled me.

I whirled us around and she yelped as I held her seated on top of me. This right here is what I wanted. My woman, riding me. Taking her pleasure out on my dick. I grunted and met her thrust for thrust, our flesh smacking, one against the other.

"Fuck, I love fucking you."

She moaned and undulated her hips, sliding up and down on my thick length. "You feel so good," she breathed as I thrust up into her, my thighs slapping her supple ass as she rode me.

"My God, yes!" She squealed as I dragged her on top of me, her tits in my face as I thrust my cock upwards, her pussy dripping all over me.

I trailed my hand to her ass, spreading her cheeks and slowly rimming her puckered hole. She cried out and tried to strain upward, but I spanked her and held her in place. With each spank, I gripped her flesh and she gripped my cock. The sex was so fucking good with this woman.

"Fuck me," she begged as I sucked on her breasts. She was now trembling above me and I flipped her around.

"You're a fucking horny slut."

"Nnngh," she moaned and spread her legs as I sunk into her. Thrust after thrust until she was crying out my name. Clenching onto my arms and running her nails down my back as she came for me. I grunted as my body responded. My balls filled up and I arched back, sinking deep inside of her as my cock exploded hot cum into her womb.

We both collapsed back onto the bed, her head falling on my arm, one leg over mine as she curled into me, giggling into my neck.

"I should be afraid of you."

I chuckled. "Why is that?"

"Cause you know exactly what to do to my body."

"And you fucking love it."

She smiled up at me. "You know I do."

I kissed the top of her head and hugged her to me. "I've got to head out tomorrow."

"For how long?"

"Just a couple of days. Need to make a shipment up into Kentucky, then I'll be back."

"I'll miss you," she whispered shyly, kissing my chest.

I played with the long locks of golden hair that covered her back, sliding my fingers through them and the thought that came to my mind was, make her yours.

"When I get back..."

"Yes," she whispered.

"You wanna be my Old Lady?"

She looked up at me, tears forming in her eyes. "You're not just saying that?"

I shook my head, curling a lock of her hair behind her ear. "I mean what I say, you know that."

I looked up at her and the tears slowly slid down her cheeks. I quickly brushed them away. "I know I don't say much but, goddamn Sadie you're etched in my fucking soul. And it's broken and dark, but you managed to dig your way right in. I don't ever want to let you go, Woman."

She smiled and leaned down to kiss me. She squealed as I hugged her tight, pressing her back into the mattress. I softly trailed a finger down her forehead, across her nose and followed the slope of her chin. "I don't believe in love, Sadie. But I do believe you were meant to come to me. I was meant to find you."

She smiled and cradled my cheek. "Well, that's good enough for me. Better than good. It's perfect. You're perfect."

"I'm far from that."

"You took care of me when no one else would, Elrik."

"I think my broken soul called out to yours, and I'm okay with that."

I looked down at her and my heart leaped. She was perfect even if she thought she wasn't. But we had our whole lives so I could teach her that lesson. The men in her life had come and gone. I eventually received my answer. While she was in the hospital she told me the truth of what had happened with Hart. How she'd used him to make Petros jealous, making it seem as if though they'd spent the night when in actuality Hart was in the shower and she'd snuck into his room knowing Petros was headed that way. He'd found her naked in Hart's bed, and that's when he saw red.

She'd made him into a fucking fool and that's when I realized that Petros' anger towards them both was justifiable. Her game had backfired, but in the end, we all benefited from it. Petros found Kinsey, Hart was with Gamble, and every move Sadie had made, led her to me. She'd begged my forgiveness but there was nothing to forgive. She made a mistake, and we've all done that at least once in our lives.

We had a long journey ahead of us, and mine had just begun. I had people I needed to take care of, and business I needed to attend to, but I also needed a good woman to warm my bed. To come home to. Someone who understood me. Sadie was beyond that and more. There was no pressure here. She wanted to be loved, but even though I didn't say the words, she still accepted me, and that was all I could give her for now.

Do I love Sadie?

In my own way, I do. And as I looked down at her bright blue eyes and flirty smile, I swore that I'd show it to her in every way I could, for the rest of her life.

Leaning over, I slid my lips over hers and kissed her. A deep penetrating kiss that only broken souls could give. One that held heavy emotions that surged through us, engulfing us and taking our breath away. Because that's exactly what she had done. She'd taken my breath away.

ROYAL BASTARDS MC SERIES

Erin Trejo: Blood Lust
Chelle C Craze & Eli Abbott: Bad Like Me
K Webster: Koyn
Esther E. Schmidt: Petros
Elizabeth Knox: Bet On Me
Glenna Maynard: Lady & the Biker
Madison Faye: Filthy Bastard
CM Genovese: Frozen Rain
J. Lynn Lombard: Blayze's Inferno
Crimson Syn: Inked In Vengeance
B.B. Blaque: Rotten Apple
Addison Jane: Her Ransom
Izzy Sweet * Sean Moriarty: Broken Wings
Nikki Landis: Ridin' For Hell
KL Ramsey: Savage Heat
M.Merin: Axel
Sapphire Knight: Bastard
Bink Cummings: Switch Burn
Winter Travers: Playboy
Linny Lawless: The Heavy Crown

Jax Hart: Desert King
Elle Boon: Royally Broken
Kristine Allen: Voodoo
Ker Dukey: Animal
KE Osborn: Defining Darkness
Shannon Youngblood: Silver & Lace

Royal Bastards MC Facebook Group - https://www.facebook.com/groups/royalbastardsmc/

RBMC Website- https://www.royalbastardsmc.com/

ABOUT THE AUTHOR

Thank you for reading!

If you enjoyed Jameson's story, please don't hesitate to leave your reviews. I do love to hear what sinful thoughts my readers throw my way!

Check out all my other series here and make sure to check out the rest of my MCs including The Hellbound Lovers & The Death Row Shooters on Amazon ...

http://bit.ly/AuthorCrimsonSyn

To get the inside scoop, teasers, new release reviews and dirty details of my upcoming series sign up for the mailing list!

My Synful Newsletter

https://bookhip.com/KLGARH

Dirty Obsession

Beautiful Betrayal

Filthy Seduction

DEATH ROW SHOOTERS MC

REAPER (Death Row Shooters MC #1)

POET (Death Row Shooters MC #2)

VINDICATOR (Death Row Shooters MC #3)

HELLBOUND LOVERS MC NOVELLAS

RYDER

BEAR

ROYAL BASTARDS MC

A Biker for Christmas

Inked for Vengeance: Royal Bastards New Orleans Chapter

A TWISTED WONDERLAND

Alice In Chains